Céad Míle
Fáilte Romhat!

(A hundred thousand welcomes to you!)

THE LITTLE BIG BOOK OF
IRELAND

Edited by
CHRISTOPHER MEASOM
and **H. CLARK WAKABAYASHI**

Designed by
TIMOTHY SHANER and
CHRISTOPHER MEASOM

welcome
BOOKS
New York • San Francisco

Published in 2007 by Welcome Books®
An imprint of Welcome Enterprises, Inc.
6 West 18th Street, New York, NY 10011
(212) 989-3200; Fax (212) 989-3205
www.welcomebooks.com

Publisher: Lena Tabori   Project Director: Alice Wong
Designed by Timothy Shaner and Christopher Measom
Project Assistants: Jeffrey McCord and Maren Gregerson
Facts & Fancy and Recipes by Christopher Measom

Library of Congress Cataloging-in-Publication Data

The little big book of Ireland / edited by Christopher Measom and H. Clark Wakabayashi;
designed by Timothy Shaner and Christopher Measom. — 1st ed.
    p. cm.
ISBN-13: 978-1-59962-021-3
ISBN-10: 1-59962-021-9
    1. Ireland—Miscellanea. I. Measom, Christopher. II. Wakabayashi, Hiro Clark, 1961–
DA906.L57 2007
941.5—dc22   2006024225

ISBN-10: 1-59962-021-9   ISBN-13: 978-1-59962-021-3

Printed in China

FIRST EDITION

3 5 7 9 10 8 6 4

CONTENTS

CONTENTS

CONTENTS

AN IRISH LIFE FOR ME

When I heard the tale gushing forth nonchalantly from my six-year-old nephew's mouth I thought, "Is it the water in Ireland?" There I was, with my father on one side and my nephew, Finn, who was visiting from Ireland, on the other. Finn was telling his grandfather—in elaborate detail no less—how he had "just *won* the basketball game outside." The fact that we hadn't played a game—just shot hoops . . . of which he hardly got any—did not deter him. My next thought was, "Is this how the legend of Finn Mac Cumhal (*page 80*) got its start?"

Okay, maybe it was more the six-year-old boy in him than the Irish. . . . Still, it made me think about what Ireland and the Irish are all about.

One thing I learned on my first trip to Ireland was that the natives seem to be genetically unable to utter the words "I don't know" when asked directions. Right or wrong, they will always tell you something, and it will *always* include a pub. I quickly found out, however, that even in the tiniest town there is never *a* pub. There is, in fact, a pub no matter which way you turn. And when I had the foresight to ask the direction giver for "the" pub's name, it became more complex: "You see, what we call McGuire's is really O'Malley's. . . ." and so the story would begin.

On my next visit I went into a convenience store and bought a road map of Dublin (smart Yank that I am), which, while not a particularly large city, can be a bit difficult to navigate—especially when relying on the guidance of the local population. The map, as it turned out, was literally bigger than the car, and I had to ask my brother to pull over so I could get out to unfold it.

But I digress (which, by the way, is a *very* Irish thing to do).

Further pondering the Irish, I considered the food as a measure of their culture.

FOREWORD

But I noticed over the past few years that instead of the more traditional meals like bacon and cabbage, the pubs are serving things like lasagna and chips. And although I find lasagna and chips to be a curiously Irish sort of combination, it is by no means what they are all about. Of course, there is also the stunning countryside, with its gorgeous ruins and long-haired cows, which does make for a romantic back-drop. But cuisine and rugged landscape aside, there is on the part of the inhabitants a certain innate talent—a mix of nimble, idosyncratic language and poignant storytelling—that strikes me as quintessentially Irish. At times it somehow manages to be clever, beautiful, bitterly sarcastic, sweet, incisive, hilarious, understated, and achingly tragic all at once.

In the excerpt from *Angela's Ashes* on page 328, Frank McCourt is able to elicit both laughter and tears while simultane-ously painting a vivid picture of the people, place, and time and adding a healthy dollop of sociopolitical color. His writing is just the latest in a long line of stunning works to come out of Ireland; but in addition to that kind of great literary talent there is the everyday Irish experience that includes—but is by no means limited to—vague yet fascinating driving directions and a six-year-old boy's cocky inventiveness.

Finally, I think George Bernard Shaw was right when he said, "An Irishman's heart is nothing but his imagination." And Shaw, I'm proud to say, was from my grandmother's hometown. . . . At least that's what she told me.

—Christopher Measom

9

FROM THE AULD SOD.

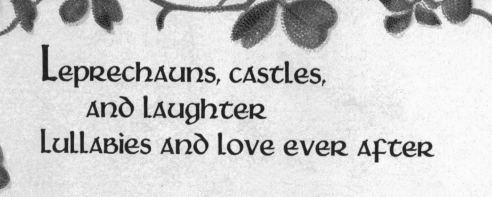

Leprechauns, castles,
and laughter
Lullabies and love ever after

With pipes and drums,
A thousand welcomes . . .
if it's the Irish you're after!

I Am of Ireland

by
Anonymous

Icham of Irlaunde
Ant of the holy londe of irlonde
Gode sir pray ich ye
for of saynte charite,
come ant daunce wyt me,
in irlaunde.

A WEE BIT O' HISTORY

As with many things Irish, there is plenty of dispute, especially over any historic "facts" that occurred before writing was introduced by St. Patrick and the Christians around the 6th century. That said, here is a very basic outline of a complex and fascinating history.

About 9500 years ago, the first people arrived in Ireland, most likely traveling on foot from Scandinavia through Scotland, eventually crossing a then-existing land bridge to settle in what is currently Antrim County.

About 8,000 years later (according to legend passed down from generation to generation), the Milesius tribe of Spain invaded, bringing Celts to the island, along with the Iron Age. Some historians suspect that the Celts were not so much invaders, however, as an aristocratic elite who moved in and lived alongside the locals, bringing their culture and language along with them.

The Gaels (an ethno-linguistic subgroup of Celts defined by the Gaelic language) became the dominant culture. (As an aside, Irish, or Gaelic, became an official language of the European Union on January 1, 2007.)

Around A.D. 80, the Roman general Agricola looked across to Ireland from Scotland (which he had just conquered) and sighed. "But a single legion would be enough for the conquest of Ireland," he said (so related the Roman historian Tacitus). However, while the rest of Celtic Europe fell to the Romans, Agricola thought Ireland was not worth the trouble, and so he let it be.

Three hundred and fifty years later, Pope Celestine I sent Palladius (who apparently had some free time after leaving his family and giving his young daughter away to a convent in Sicily, but that's another story) to Ireland to be the first bishop of "the Irish that believe in Christ"—who were few and far between in those days, Druids being much more common.

A year later, a lad—formerly named Maewyn Succat—was also sent to Ireland by Pope Celestine I to spread Christianity throughout the land. Maewyn, who had been a slave/shepherd to a Druidical high priest until an angel encouraged him to escape, often had visions of returning to Erin while he was studying Christianity in France. He took a new name (Patrick) and after about 40 years of missionary work in Ireland, he succeeded in converting a great many citizens. Now known as St. Patrick, he also became the patron Saint of Ireland, New York, and Poona, India, amongst other things.

Peace, calm, and scholarship abounded from St. Patrick's time until a.d. 795, when the Vikings arrived. Although they did some good—founding Dublin, for example, and introducing the idea of coinage (replacing the

ronar buan

A Wee Bit o' History

ERINS ISLE

Catholic rebellion and reassert English rule and Protestantism.

In 1759 Arthur Guinness bought a brewery in Dublin.

In Georgian Ireland (under England's George III), the Protestants got richer—providing the island with gorgeous manor houses—while the Catholics were denied even the right to purchase land.

The history of 19th-century Ireland is dominated by a relatively brief but deadly occurrence—the famine of 1845–1848. In the following 50 years, Ireland's population dropped (through death and emigration) from 8 million to 4 million. Ireland's loss (sad as it was) became America's gain.

In 1921, the Anglo-Irish Treaty was signed, leaving the island split between the Irish Free State (now known as the Republic of Ireland, or just plain Ireland) and Northern Ireland (a state within the United Kingdom). The country plunged into an 11-month civil war.

The "Troubles"—grueling, sporadic, guerrilla warfare between the Catholics and

cow as legal tender)—they pillaged a lot, too. Still, over the next 150 years they managed to assimilate into Irish society, taking on Irish wives, Christianity, and even Celtic surnames.

In 1169, the Anglo-Normans, led by a Welsh archer known as Strongbow, arrived. Eight centuries of on-again, off-again English-Irish struggle ensued.

It was in 1649, as the struggles waxed and waned, that the much hated and ruthless Lord Oliver Cromwell arrived to put down the

A Wee Bit o' History

Protestants in Northern Ireland—lasted from the 1960s to the 1990s. The Irish Republican Army declared a cease-fire in 1994, and in 1998 a peace plan was accepted by all, ending the "Troubles." Still, the occasional rock is tossed.

On January 1, 2002, Ireland adopted the euro as its common currency, replacing the Irish punt, which somewhere through the years replaced Viking coinage, which had replaced the cow. ☘

MERCIER AND CAMIER

BY SAMUEL BECKETT

A road still carriageable climbs over the high moorland. It cuts across vast turf bogs, a thousand feet above sea-level, two thousand if you prefer. It leads to nothing any more. A few ruined forts, a few ruined dwellings. The sea is not far, just visible beyond the valleys dipping eastward, pale plinth as pale as the pale wall of sky. Tarns lie hidden in the folds of the moor, invisible from the road, reached by faint paths, under high overhanging crags. All seems flat, or gently undulating, and there at a stone's throw these high crags, all unsuspected by the wayfarer. Of granite what is more. In the west the chain is at its highest, its peaks exalt even the most downcast eyes, peaks commanding the vast champaign land, the celebrated pastures, the golden vale. Before the travellers, as far as the eye can reach, the road winds on into the south, uphill, but imperceptibly. None ever pass this way

but beauty-spot hogs and fanatical trampers. Under its heather mask the quag allures, with an allurement not all mortals can resist. Then it swallows them up or the mist comes down. The city is not far either, from certain points its lights can be seen by night, its light rather, and by day its haze. Even the piers of the harbor can be distinguished, on very clear days, of the two harbors, tiny arms in the glassy sea outflung, known flat, seen raised. And the islands and promontories, one has only to stop and turn at the right place, and of course by night the beacon lights, both flashing and revolving. It is here one would lie down, in a hollow bedded with dry heather, and fall asleep, for the last time, on an afternoon, in the sun, head down among the minute life of stems and bells, and fast fall asleep, fast farewell to charming things. It's a birdless sky, the odd raptor, no song. End of descriptive passage. ●

SAMUEL BECKETT (1906–1989). Best known for his stark, fragmented plays, Beckett also wrote poetry and novels. Above all, however, he was a writer of the 20th century moving away (at a rapid pace) from traditional realism to modernism. Plot, time, place, and even dialogue were not fundamental to his work. About *Waiting for Godot*, the critic Vivian Mercier wrote in the *Irish Times* that Beckett "has achieved a theoretical impossibility—a play in which nothing happens, that yet keeps audiences glued to their seats."

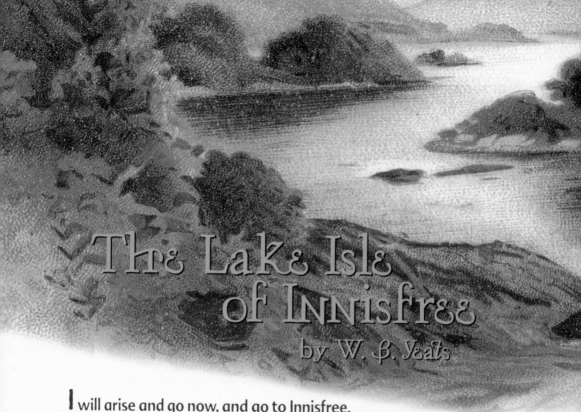

The Lake Isle of Innisfree
by W. B. Yeats

I will arise and go now, and go to Innisfree,
And a small cabin build there, of clay and wattles made:
Nine bean-rows will I have there, a hive for the honey-bee,
And live alone in the bee-loud glade.

And I shall have some peace there, for peace comes dropping slow,
Dropping from the veils of the morning to where the cricket sings;

There midnight's all a glimmer, and noon a purple glow,
And evening full of the linnet's wings.

I will arise and go now, for always night and day
I hear lake water lapping with low sounds by the shore;
While I stand on the roadway, or on the pavements grey,
I hear it in the deep heart's core.

21

THE PERFECT POT OF TAY
(IN IRISH, "CUPAN TAE")

*T*here is a saying in Ireland that a proper cup of tea should be "strong enough for a mouse to trot on." I'm not sure what that means exactly, but I do know that the Irish love their tea. In fact, they drink more tea per capita than any other nation in the world. And although most Irish use the electric kettle and tea bags nowadays, this is how a "proper" cup is made.

Teakettle
Cold water (from the tap is best
    because it's aerated)
Porcelain or earthenware teapot
Irish breakfast blend: 3 parts Assam,
    1 part Ceylon or Afternoon Blend
    (2 parts Darjeeling, 1 part Assam,
    1 part Ceylon, 1 part Keemun)
Whole milk
Tea strainer
Tea cozy or tea towel
Sugar, cubed, coarse, or in packets

1. Put the kettle on to boil. When the water boils, pour a small amount of the hot water into the teapot and swirl to warm the pot. Discard the water.
2. Put the loose tea leaves into the teapot. Use 1 heaping teaspoon per cup of water, then add 1 extra "for the pot." Stir gently, then let steep for 5 minutes.
3. Fill each teacup a quarter to a third of the way up with milk. This must be done *before* pouring the tea.
4. Place the tea strainer over each teacup as you pour. After serving, cover the teapot with a cozy or tea towel to keep it warm. Add sugar to taste.
5. Use the old tea leaves to feed your roses or other acid-loving plants.

The Birth of Cuchulain

The following passage, translated and retold by Lady Gregory, is of the birth of the legendary Cuchulain, Champion of Ireland—an Irish Achilles who was the greatest of ancient Ireland's fabled Knights of the Red Branch.

And when they had eaten and drunk and began to be satisfied, Conchubar said to the young man: "Where is the mistress of the house that she does not come to bid us welcome?" "You cannot see her tonight," said he, "for she is in the pains of childbirth." So they rested there that night, and in the morning Conchubar was the first to rise up; but he saw no more of the man of the house, and what he heard was the cry of a child. And he went to the room it came from, and there he saw Dechtire, and her maidens about her, and a young child beside her. And she bade Conchubar welcome, and she told him all that had happened her, and that she had called him there to bring herself and the child back to Emain Macha. And Conchubar said: "It is well you have done by me, Dechtire; you gave shelter to me and to my chariots; you kept the cold from my horses; you gave food to me and my people, and

The Birth of Cuchulain

now you have given us this good gift. And let our sister, Finchoem, bring up the child," he said. "No, it is not for her to bring him up, it is for me," said Sencha son of Ailell, chief judge and chief poet of Ulster. "For I am skilled; I am good in disputes; I am not forgetful; I speak before any one at all in the presence of the king; I watch over what he says; I give judgment in the quarrels of kings; I am judge of the men of Ulster; no one has a right to dispute my claim, but only Conchubar."

"If the child is given to me to bring up," said Blai, the distributer, "he will not suffer from want of care or from forgetfulness. It is my messages that do the will of Conchubar; I call up the fighting men from all Ireland; I am well able to provide for them for a week, or even for ten days; I settle their business and their disputes; I support their honor; I get satisfaction for their insults."

"You think too much of yourself," said Fergus. "It is I that will bring up the child; I am strong; I have knowledge; I am the king's messenger; no one can stand up against me in honor or riches; I am hardened to war and battles; I am a good craftsman; I am worthy to bring up a child. I am the protector of all the unhappy; the strong are afraid of me; I am the helper of the weak."

The Birth of Cuchulain

"If you will listen to me at last, now you are quiet," said Amergin, "I am able to bring up a child like a king. The people praise my honor, my bravery, my courage, my wisdom; they praise my good luck, my age, my speaking, my name, my courage, and my race. Though I am a fighter, I am a poet; I am worthy of the king's favor; I overcome all the men who fight from their chariots; I owe thanks to no one except Conchubar; I obey no one but the king."

Then Sencha said: "Let Finchoem keep the child until we come to Emain, and Morann, the judge, will settle the question when we are there."

So the men of Ulster set out for Emain, Finchoem having the child with her. And when they came there Morann gave his judgment. "It is for Conchubar," he said, "to help the child to a good name, for he is next of kin to him; let Sencha teach him words and speaking; let Fergus hold him on his knees; let Amergin be his tutor." And he said: "This child will be praised by all, by chariot drivers and fighters, by kings and by wise men; he shall be loved by many men; he will avenge all your wrongs; he will defend your fords; he will fight all your battles."

FACTS & FANCY
NATURAL WONDERS

THE ARAN ISLANDS (County Galway) So foreboding is the landscape that islanders had to make their own soil out of seaweed and rocks. J. M. Synge captured the bleakness in his plays. Today you can tour by minibus or bike. Look for prehistoric stone forts, currachs, and the famous sweaters.

THE BURREN (County Clare) *Burren* means "rocky land" in Gaelic. A general under the not-so-nice-to-the-Irish Oliver Cromwell described the area this way: "A savage land, yielding neither water enough to drown a man, nor tree to hang him, nor soil enough to bury." Look for the pearl-bordered fritillary and the hoary rook rose. The nearby village of Doolin is known for its traditional music.

CLIFFS OF MOHER (County Clare) At a height of 230 meters above the raging Atlantic, these cliffs boast the most amazing view of Ireland. Along the "brilliant" cliff walks, look for guillemots and kittiwakes.

DINGLE PENINSULA (County Kerry) A series of cliffs and beautiful seascapes dotted with rocky islands, this is one of the most scenic coastlines of Europe. Look for beehive huts, Dunbeg Fort, and choughs.

THE MOUNTAINS OF MOURNE (County Down) *Mountain* is lyrical Irish for "tallish hill," (these top out around 2,000 feet). Rent a bike in Newcastle and ride to Carlingford Lough, stopping at Green Castle.

RING OF GULLION (County Armagh) The beautiful heather-clad *slieve* Gullion is surrounded by a "ring" of low hills. This area is associated with lots of Ireland's legends and myths. Look for stories about Cuchulainn and Finn MacCool.

RING OF KERRY (County Kerry) Since this is one of the most visited sights in the country, it is best to arrive early to beat the tour buses. Along the circular, or "ring," road around the

Iveragh Peninsula that makes up the Ring of Kerry, look for the charming village Sneem, Moll's Gap, and the Macgillicuddy's Reeks.

SHANNON RIVER Ireland's largest river runs from Northwest County Cavan through centrally located Limerick and out to the Atlantic. Stunning vistas, fishing, boating, castles, and charming villages can be found along the way. Look for water lobelia and the great crested grebe.

WICKLOW MOUNTAINS (County Wicklow) Less than an hour from Dublin but light-years away from the hustle and bustle lie these wild, rugged mountains. Drive the Military Road and look for Glendalough, Vale of Avoca, and locally made woven goods.

THE BOGS OF IRELAND Located typically in the midlands and composed of organic materials compressed over millennia, bogs yield peat, or "turf," which is used as fuel. Once experienced, the unique aromatic smell of a turf fire is never forgotten. Look for bog oaks, a *slane*, and the four-spotted dragonfly.

GIANT'S CAUSEWAY (County Antrim)
This is Ireland's first World Heritage site, and of course, ho-hum "volcanic activity" would never do to explain the 40,000 hexagonal basalt columns spectacularly leading into the sea. No, it was the giant Finn MacCool.

Prelude

by J. M. Synge

Still south I went and west and south again,
Through Wicklow from the morning till the night,
And far from cities, and the sites of men,
Lived with the sunshine and the moon's delight.

I knew the stars, the flowers, and the birds,
The grey and wintry sides of many glens,
And did but half remember human words,
In converse with the mountains, moors, and fens.

THE LONG ROAD TO UMMERA

BY FRANK O'CONNOR

"Musha, take me back to Ummera, Pat," she whined. "Take me back to my own. I'd never rest among strangers. I'd be rising and drifting."

"Ah, foolishness, woman!" he said with an indignant look. "That sort of thing is gone out of fashion."

"I won't stop here for you," she shouted hoarsely in sudden, impotent fury, and she rose and grasped the mantelpiece for support.

"You won't be asked," he said shortly.

"I'll haunt you," she whispered tensely, holding on to the mantelpiece and bending down over him with a horrible grin.

"And that's only more of the foolishness," he said with a nod of contempt. "Haunts and fairies and spells."

She took one step towards him and stood, plastering down the two little locks of yellowing hair, the half-dead eyes twitching and blinking in the candlelight, and the swollen crumpled face with the cheeks like cracked enamel.

"Pat," she said, "the day we left Ummera you promised to bring me back. You were only a little gorsoon that time. The neighbors gathered round me and the last word I said to them and I going down the road was: 'Neighbors, my son Pat is after

giving me his word and he'll bring me back to ye when my time comes.' ... That's as true as the Almighty God is over me this night. I have everything ready." She went to the shelf under the stairs and took out two parcels. She seemed to be speaking to herself as she opened them gloatingly, bending down her head in the feeble light of the candle. "There's the two brass candlesticks and the blessed candles alongside them. And there's my shroud aired regular on the line."

"Ah, you're mad, woman," he said angrily. "Forty miles! Forty miles into the heart of the mountains!"

She suddenly shuffled towards him on her bare feet, her hand raised clawing the air, her body like her face blind with age. Her harsh croaking old voice rose to a shout.

"I brought you from it, boy, and you must bring me back. If 'twas the last shilling you had and you and your children to go to the poorhouse after, you must bring me back to Ummera. And not by the short road either! Mind what I say now! The long road! The long road to Ummera round the lake, the way I brought you from it. I lay a heavy curse on you this night if you bring me the short road over the hill. And ye must stop by the ash tree at the foot of the boreen where ye can see my little house and say a prayer for all that were ever old in it and all that played on the floor. And then—Pat! Pat Driscoll! Are you listening? Are you listening to me, I say?"

THE LONG ROAD TO UMMERA

She shook him by the shoulder, peering down into his long miserable face to see how was he taking it.

"I'm listening," he said with a shrug.

"Then"—her voice dropped to a whisper—"you must stand up overright the neighbors and say—remember now what I'm telling you!—'Neighbors, this is Abby, Batty Heige's daughter, that kept her promise to ye at the end of all.'"

She said it lovingly, smiling to herself, as if it were a bit of an old song, something she went over and over in the long night. All West Cork was in it: the bleak road over the moors to Ummera, the smooth gray pelts of the hills with the long spider's web of the fences ridging them, drawing the scarecrow fields awry, and the whitewashed cottages, poker-faced between their little scraps of holly bushes looking this way and that out of the wind . . .

FRANK O'CONNOR (1903–1966) was the pseudonym of Michael O'Donovan, who was born in Cork in poverty, self-educated, and fought on the Republican side in the War of Independence. He was interned at Gormanstown in 1923, which informed much of his later writing. After his release, he became a librarian and moved from Wicklow to Cork to Dublin, where he met W. B. Yeats and George Russell. He wrote stories, novels, poetry, plays, and translations prolifically.

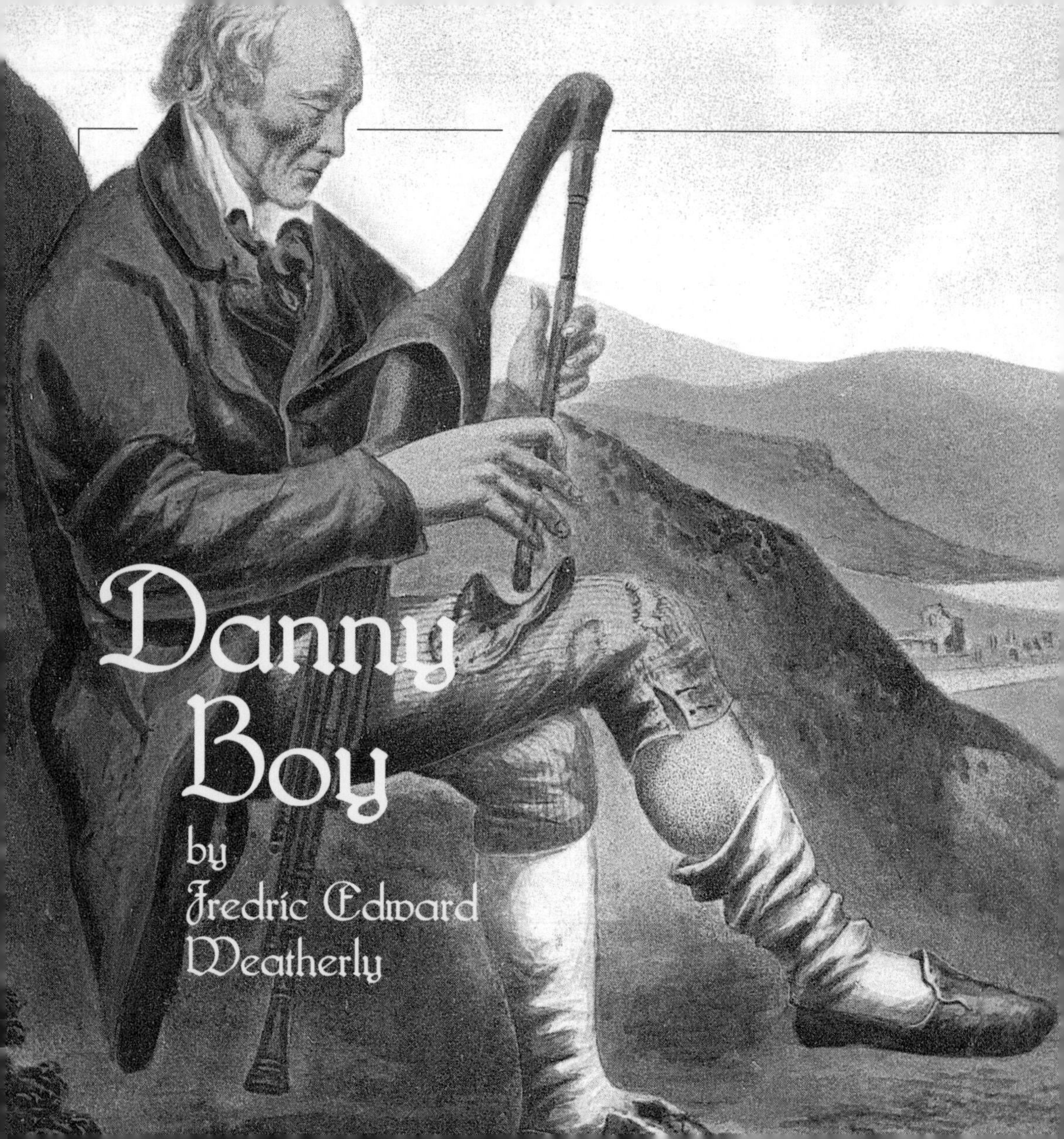

Danny Boy

by
Fredric Edward
Weatherly

Oh, Danny Boy the pipes, the pipes are calling
From glen to glen, and down the mountain side,
The summer's gone, and all the roses falling,
It's you, it's you must go, and I must bide.

But come ye back when summer's in the meadow,
Or when the valley's hushed and white with snow,
It's I'll be here in sunshine or in shadow,
Oh, Danny Boy, oh, Danny Boy, I love you so!

But when ye come, and all the flow'rs are dying,
If I am dead, as dead I well may be,
Ye'll come and find the place where I am lying,
And kneel and say an Ave there for me;

And I shall hear, tho' soft you tread above me,
And all my grave will warmer, sweeter be,
For you will bend and tell me that you love me,
And I shall sleep in peace until you come to me!

NOTE: Many are surprised to hear that this quintessentially Irish song isn't actually Irish—at least the lyrics aren't. They were written by an Englishman. There is evidence, however, that the melody is by a blind harper and clan chieftain named Rory Dall O'Cahan. The story goes that Rory—due to the pain of being removed from his ancestral land by English settlers in 1609—had a few too many, fell in a ditch, and awoke to the sound of angels playing what we now know as *Danny Boy*. Whatever the origins, this touching, evocative piece seldom fails to wrench a tear from anyone with even a drop of Irish in him.

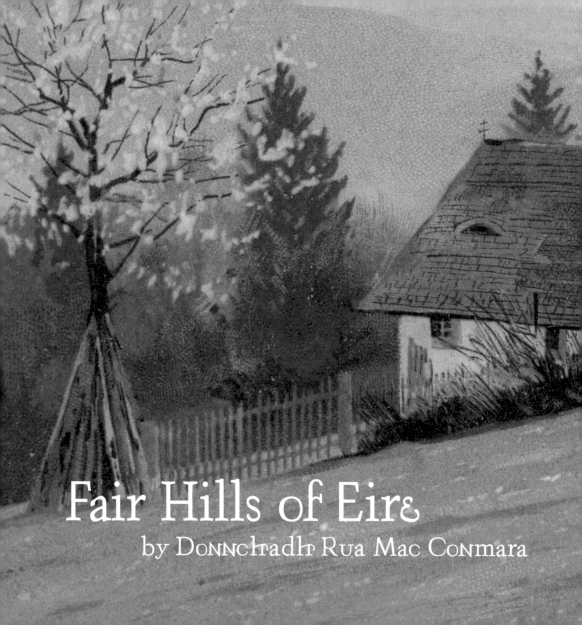

Fair Hills of Eire

by Donnchradh Rua Mac Conmara

Take my heart's blessing over to dear Eire's strand—
    Fair Hills of Eire O!
To the Remnant that love her—Our Forefathers' Land!
    Fair Hills of Eire O!
How sweet sing the birds, o'er mount there and vale,
Like soft-sounding chords, that lament for the Gael,—
And I, o'er the surge, far, far away must wail
    The Fair Hills of Eire O.

EMERALD ISLE GEMS

The Irish flag—called the "Tricolour" for its green, white and orange stripes—was designed in 1848. Its meaning is still relevant today: the green stands for Irish Catholics and one united country, the orange stands for Irish Protestants, and the white between represents the hope for peace.

When Captian Charles Boycott refused his Co. Mayo tenants' request for lower rent in 1880 then ejected them for askingthey protested by refusing to work his land or do business with him—thus the word *boycott*.

Some English words plucked from Irish include galore, hooligan, hubbub, phony, slop, and smithereens. Words that can be traced phonetically from Irish include swell from *sóúil* (luxurious), abracadabra from *aithbhreith cad aithhreith* (the act of regenerating), and highfalutin' from *uí bhfolaíocht án* (descended from noble blood).

St. Valentine may have lived and died in Rome, but his remains (at least some of them) are located in the Whitefriar Street Carmelite Church in Dublin. Back in 1835 Pope Gregory XVI ordered the saint exhumed from St. Hippolytus cemetery near Rome and—as a token of thanks—gave them to Carmelite priest John Spratt in Ireland.

The phrase "the Emerald Isle" first appeared in print in the poem "Erin" written by radical patriot Dr. William Drennan in 1795.

The leprechaun has been described as Ireland's national fairy. Its ancient origins are from a great Euro-Celtic sun god named Lugh (pronounced luck). The word leprechaun is derived from the Irish *luchorpan,* meaning little body. Leprechauns are rarely more than two feet tall and look like old men. They are shoemakers by trade, and are easily identified by the shamrock in their

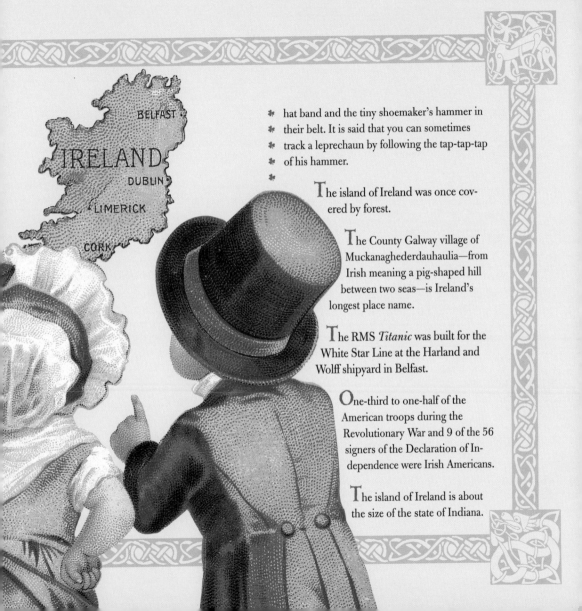

hat band and the tiny shoemaker's hammer in their belt. It is said that you can sometimes track a leprechaun by following the tap-tap-tap of his hammer.

The island of Ireland was once covered by forest.

The County Galway village of Muckanaghederdauhaulia—from Irish meaning a pig-shaped hill between two seas—is Ireland's longest place name.

The RMS *Titanic* was built for the White Star Line at the Harland and Wolff shipyard in Belfast.

One-third to one-half of the American troops during the Revolutionary War and 9 of the 56 signers of the Declaration of Independence were Irish Americans.

The island of Ireland is about the size of the state of Indiana.

We have always found the Irish a bit odd. They refuse to be English.

—Winston Churchill

The Leprehaun
by Lady Francesca Speranza Wilde

The Leprehauns are merry, industrious, tricksy little sprites, who do all the shoemaker's work and the tailor's and the cobbler's for the fairy gentry, and are often seen at sunset under the hedge singing and stitching. They know all the secrets of hidden treasure, and if they take a fancy to a person will guide him to the spot in the fairy rath where the pot of gold lies buried. It is believed that a family now living near Castlerea came by their riches in a strange way, all through the good offices of a friendly Leprehaun. And the legend has been handed down through many generations as an established fact.

There was a poor boy once, one of their forefathers, who used to drive his cart of turf daily back and forward, and make what money be could by the sale; but he was a strange boy, very silent and moody, and the people said he was a fairy changeling, for he joined in no sports and scarcely ever spoke to any one, but spent the nights reading all the old bits of books he picked up in

The Leprehaun

his rambles. The one thing he longed for above all others was to get rich, and to be able to give up the old weary turf cart, and live in peace and quietness all alone, with nothing but books round him, in a beautiful house and garden all by himself.

Now he had read in the old books how the Leprehauns knew all the secret places where gold lay hid, and day by day he watched for a sight of the little cobbler, and listened for the click, click of his hammer as he sat under the hedge mending the shoes.

At last, one evening just as the sun set, he saw a little fellow under a dock leaf, working away, dressed all in green, with a cocked hat on his head. So the boy jumped down from the cart and seized him by the neck.

"Now, you don't stir from this," he cried, "till you tell me where to find the hidden gold."

"Easy now," said the Leprehaun, "don't hurt me, and I will tell you all about it. But mind you, I could hurt you if I chose, for I have the power; but I won't do it, for we are cousins once removed. So as we are near relations I'll just be good, and show you the place of the secret gold that none can have or keep

The Leprehaun

except those of fairy blood and race. Come along with me, then, to the old fort of Lipenshaw, for there it lies. But make haste, for when the last red glow of the sun vanishes the gold will disappear also, and you will never find it again."

"Come off, then," said the boy, and he carried the Leprehaun into the turf cart, and drove off. And in a second they were at the old fort, and went in through a door made in the stone wall.

"Now, look around," said the Leprehaun; and the boy saw the whole ground covered with gold pieces, and there were vessels of silver lying about in such plenty that all the riches of all the world seemed gathered there.

"Now take what you want," said the Leprehaun, "but hasten, for if that door shuts you will never leave this place as long as you live."

So the boy gathered up his arms full of gold and silver, and flung them into the cart; and was on his way back for more when the door shut with a clap like thunder, and all the place became dark as night. And he saw no more of the Leprehaun, and had not time even to thank him.

The Leprehaun

So he thought it best to drive home at once with his treasure, and when he arrived and was all alone by himself he counted his riches, and all the bright yellow gold pieces, enough for a king's ransom.

And he was very wise and told no one; but went off next day to Dublin and put all his treasures into the bank, and found that he was now indeed as rich as a lord.

So he ordered a fine house to be built with spacious gardens, and he had servants and carriages and books to his heart's content. And he gathered all the wise men round him to give him the learning of a gentleman; and he became a great and powerful man in the country, where his memory is still held in high honour, and his descendants are living to this day rich and prosperous; for their wealth has never decreased though they have ever given largely to the poor, and are noted above all things for the friendly heart and the liberal hand.

Boxty (Irish Potato Griddle Cakes)

Boxty on the griddle,
Boxty in the pan,
If you can't make boxty,
You'll never get a man.

If this recipe doesn't work out for you and you still want a man, there's always the Lisdoonvarna Matchmaking Festival in County Clare (see page 103) . . .

2 cups grated raw potatoes
2 cups leftover mashed potatoes
2 cups all-purpose flour
2 teaspoons baking powder
2 teaspoons salt
Ground pepper to taste
2 eggs, beaten
$1/4$–$1/2$ cup milk (more or less as
    needed)
1 tablespoon butter or oil
    (or more as needed)

1. Mix together the raw and mashed potatoes.
2. Sift together the flour, baking powder, salt, and pepper, then add to the potatoes. Stir in the beaten eggs, mixing thoroughly.
3. Add the milk until it makes a batter.
4. Drop by the tablespoonful onto a hot buttered or oiled frying pan and cook over moderate heat until browned (3 to 4 minutes per side). Serve hot with butter or a tart applesauce.

Yield: 6 servings.

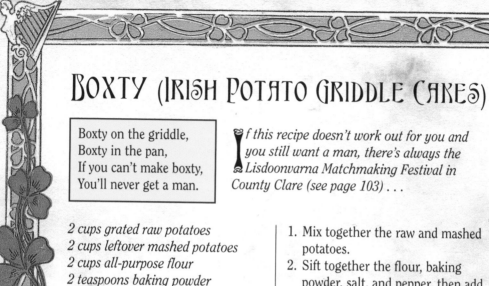

50

FACTS & FANCY
TOUR-A-LOORING

Renting a car and staying in Ireland's famous B&Bs is one of the most popular ways to visit the Emerald Isle. You will meet people in their own home, wake up to a home-cooked full Irish breakfast and, without question, get lost along the way. Here are some other fun ideas for touring.

BARGES Rent a barge and cruise the Shannon or the Grand Canal at a leisurely pace. Just don't set sail after a "knees-up" at the local.

BIKING Pedaling through the countryside gives you a chance to stop and moo at a cow or pick the wild blackberries from the overflowing bushes at the side of the road.

CASTLES Live like a king . . . with central heating. Many castles in Ireland—some as old as 900 years—have been made into modern-day hotels, while retaining their original character.

EQUESTRIAN Over rolling parkland or along the strands of the Atlantic, "horse riding" through unspoiled Ireland is as old as the hills.

FISHING Irish trout and salmon have had anglers after them for centuries. Fish Oorid Lough, Ballynahinch Lake, or the Shannon.

FOLKLORE AND MYTHOLOGY Ireland's rich culture includes plenty of sacred sites, Celtic spirituality, traditional music, and storytellers and singers to walk you through them.

GARDENS Whether you prefer the public botanic gardens or the old estates of the landed gentry, Ireland's mild and moist climate makes for spectacular greenery.

GOLF Play some of Europe's most famous courses like Ballybunion, Druid's Glen, and Adare Manor. Watch out for the sheep!

LITERARY Visit the places Erin's writers lived in and wrote about. Bring their famous and infamous works with you for reference.

MANOR HOUSES Some of the best food in the country is found on the tables of these charming guesthouses. Many grow their own organic produce in the back garden, too.

WALKING/HIKING The antithesis of the big bus tour, there's nothing like a walk across the Emerald Isle. Who knows? You may catch a leprechaun!

WRITING COURSE If you are the next James Joyce, spend a week brushing up on your writing skills. If you are simply Joyce James, however, you might want to take in a lecture or two on your favorite Irish scribe instead.

THE IRISH SKETCHBOOK

BY WILLIAM MAKEPEACE THACKERAY

O you who laboriously throw flies in English rivers, and catch, at the expiration of a hard day's walking, casting, and wading, two or three feeble little brown trouts of two or three ounces in weight, how would you rejoice to have put an hour's sport in Derryclear or Ballinahinch; where you have but to cast, and lo! a big trout springs at your fly, and, after making a vain struggling, splashing, and plunging for a while, is infallibly landed in the net and thence into the boat. The single rod in the boat caught enough fish in an hour to feast the crew, consisting of five persons, and the family of a herd of Mr. Martin's who has a pretty cottage on Derryclear Lake, inhabited by a cow and its calf, a score of fowls, and I don't know how many sons and daughters.

Having caught enough trout to satisfy any moderate appetite, like true sportsmen the gentlemen on board our boat became eager to hook a salmon. Had they hooked a few salmon, no doubt they would have trolled for whales, or for a mermaid; one of which finny beauties the waterman swore he had seen on the shore of Derryclear—he with Jim Mullen being above on a rock, the mermaid on the shore directly beneath them, visible to the middle, and as usual "racking her hair." It was fair hair, the boatman said; and he appeared as convinced of the existence of the mermaid as he was of the trout just landed in the boat.

In regard of mermaids, there is a gentleman living near Killala Bay, whose name was mentioned to me, and who declares solemnly that one day, shooting on the sands there, he saw a mermaid, and determined to try her with a shot. So he drew the small charge from his gun and loaded it with ball—that he always had for him for seal-shooting—fired, and hit the mermaid through the breast. The screams and moans of the creature—whose person he describes most accurately—were the most horrible, heart-rending noises that he ever, he said, heard; and not only were they heard by him, but by the fishermen along the coast, who were furiously angry against Mr. A——n, because, they said, the injury done to the mermaid would cause her to drive all the fish away from the bay for years to come.

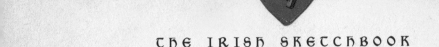

But we did not, to my disappointment, catch a glimpse of one of these interesting beings, nor of the great sea-horse which is said to inhabit these waters, nor of any fairies (of whom the stroke-oar, Mr. Marcus, told us not to speak, for they didn't like bein' spoken of); nor even of a salmon, though the fishermen produced the most tempting flies. The only animal of any size that was visible we saw while lying

by a swift black river that comes jumping with innumerable little waves into Derryclear, and where the salmon are especially suffered to "stand": this animal was an eagle—a real wild eagle, with gray wings and a white head and belly: it swept round us, within gunshot reach, once or twice, through the leaden sky, and then settled on a gray rock and began to scream its shrill ghastly aquiline note.

The attempts of the salmon having failed, the rain continuing to fall steadily, the herd's cottage before named was resorted to: when Marcus, the boatman, commenced forthwith to gut the fish, and taking down some charred turf-ashes from the glazing fire, on which about a hundredweight of potatoes were boiling, he—Marcus—proceeded to grill on the floor some of the trout, which we afterwards ate with immeasurable satisfaction. They were such trouts as, when once tasted, remain forever in the recollection of a commonly grateful mind—rich, flaky, creamy, full of flavor. A Parisian *gourmand* would have paid ten francs for the smallest *cooleen* among them; and, when transported to his capital, how different in flavor would they have been!—how inferior to what they were as we devoured them, fresh from the fresh waters of the lake, and jerked as it were from the water to the gridiron! The world had not had time to spoil those innocent beings before they were gobbled up with pepper and salt, and missed, no doubt, by their friends. I should like to know more of their "*set*." But enough of this: my feelings overpower me: suffice it to say, they were red or salmon trouts—none of your white-fleshed brown-skinned river fellows.

When the gentlemen had finished their repast, the boatmen and the family set to work upon the ton of potatoes, a number of the remaining fish, and a store of other good things; then we all sat round the turf-fire in the dark cottage, the rain coming down steadily outside, and veiling everything execpt the shrubs and verdure immediately about the cottage. The herd, the herd's wife, and a nondescript female friend, two healthy young herdsmen in corduroy rags, the herdsman's daughter paddling about with bare feet, a stout black-eyed wench with her gown over her head and a red petticoat not quite so good as new, the two boatmen, a badger just killed and turned inside out, the gentlemen, some hens cackling and flapping about among the rafters, a calf in a corner cropping green meat and occasionally visited by the cow her mamma, formed the society of the place. It was rather a strange picture; but as for about tow hours we sat there, and maintained an almost unbroken silence, and as there was no other amusement but to look at the rain, I began, after the enthusiasm of the first half-hour to think that after all London was a bearable place, and that for want of a turf-fire and a bench in Connemara, one *might* put up with a sofa and a newspaper in Pall Mall.

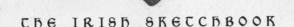

This, however, is according to tastes; and I must say that Mr. Marcus betrayed a most bitter contempt for all cockney tastes, awkwardness, and ignorance: and very right too. The night, on our return home, all of a sudden cleared; but though the fishermen, much to my disgust—at the expression of which, however, the rascals only laughed—persisted in making more casts for trout, and trying back in the dark upon the spots which we had visited in the morning, it appeared the fish had been frightened off by the rain; and the sportsmen met with such indifferent success that at about ten o'clock we found ourselves at Ballinahinch. Dinner was served at eleven, and, I believe, there was some whiskey-punch afterwards, recommended medicinally and to prevent the ill effects of the wetting: but that is neither here nor there. ●

WILLIAM MAKEPEACE THACKERAY (1811–1863). Born in Calcutta, India, to British-Indian parents, Thackeray is known not only as a great novelist but also as a brilliant satirist. In 1848 he achieved widespread popularity with his humorous *Book of Snobs* and the same year rose to major rank among English novelists with *Vanity Fair*. *The Irish Sketchbook* glimpses into his lesser-known but skillfully beautiful travel writing.

So I have come into Wicklow, where the fields are sharply green, where a wild beauty hides in the glens, where sudden surprising vistas open up as the road rises and falls; and here i smell for the first time the incense of ireland, the smoke of turf fires, and here for the first time i see the face of the irish countryside.

—H. V. Morton
from *In Search of Ireland*

The Sea Fairies

by Patrick Kennedy

Moruadh, or *Moruach*, is the name given to the mer–maids that haunt the shallow waters near our coasts. The word is composed of *Mur*, sea, and *Oich*, maid. The mermen do not seem on the whole to be an attractive or interesting class. Their hair and, teeth are green, their noses invariably red, and their eyes resemble those of a pig. Moreover, they have a penchant for brandy, and keep a lookout for cases of that article that go astray in shipwrecks. Some naturalists attribute the hue of their noses to extra indulgence in that liquor. It is little to be wondered at that their young women occasionally prefer marriage with a coast farmer. The wearing of a nice little magic cap (the *Cohuleen Druith*) is essential to their well-being in their country below the waves, and the mortal husband must keep this cap well concealed from his sea-wife, instances are rife of desolation made in families by the inadvertent finding of it by one of the children, who, of course, shows it to his mother to learn what it is.

The Sea Fairies

However strong her affection for husband and children, she is instinctively obliged to seize on it, and clap it on her head. She tenderly embraces her children, but immediately flies to the sea-brink, plunges in, and is seen no more. The distracted husband, when he hears the news from the forsaken children, accuses destiny, and calls for aid to the powers of sea and land, but all in vain. Why did he perpetrate an unsuitable marriage?

One man, who lived near Bantry, was blessed with an excellent wife of this class. (As a rule, a Moruach is most desirable as wife, mother, and mistress of a family.) They would have lived comfortably, but many sea-cows, aware of her original condition, would persist in coming up to graze on her husband's meadows, and thus be near their relative. The husband, an unsentimental fellow, would chase and worry the poor sea-cattle, even to wounds and bruises, till the wife, after many useless appeals to his good feelings, poked out her Cohuleen Druith and quitted him. He was sorry when it was too late. His children, and theirs again, were distinguished by a rough scaly skin and a delicate membrane between fingers and toes.

FACTS & FANCY
NOT-SO-NATURAL WONDERS

BANTRY HOUSE AND GARDENS
(County Cork) A dramatic and stately example of an Irish country house, it is still occupied by the descendents of the Earls of Bantry. You, too, can stay there. In the garden look for the "Hundred Steps," surrounded by azaleas and rhododendron.

THE BOOK OF KELLS (Trinity College, Dublin) Named after the monastery in the town of Kells, where the book resided for at least 500 years, it is now housed in Trinity College, Dublin. This illustrated biblical text is a masterpiece. Note the unusual use of many colors, including lilac, pink, red, green, and lapis lazuli.

CLONMACNOISE (County Offaly) Three very well preserved High Crosses can be seen amongst the ruins of this early Christian Monastic settlement. Look for the crozier of the Abbots of Clonmacnoise.

CRANNOGS Look closely, and in many lakes you will see the remnants of ancient crannogs, or artificial islands. After 3,000 years, one might look a bit like a beaver's lodge. First used for fishing; later becoming safe havens for living.

DOLMEN These megalithic tombs can be spotted almost anywhere in the countryside—often in such random places as a hedged-in cow pasture. Look for unnaturally stacked flat rocks in the shape of a giant picnic table.

THE HILL OF TARA (County Meath) This is the ancient seat of both spiritual and political power in Ireland. The mythology is that the

OGHAM STONES These ancient pillar-like stones are found scattered throughout the country, mainly in the southwest. They can be identified by the lines (*ogham*) carved into the corners of the stones. These are actually letters from an ancient Celtic alphabet.

ancient gods dwelled here. More recently—until the 12th century—the high kings lived, ruled, and were buried here. Look for the phallic "stone of destiny" and the statue of St. Patrick, representing the shift in power to the Catholic Church.

NEWGRANGE (County Meath) This impressive passage tomb, decorated with pre-Celtic Irish swirls, is located in the Boyne Valley (sometimes referred to as the Irish Valley of the Kings, although it is older than the one in Egypt). Legend has it that the High Kings of Tara were buried here. For several days at the winter solstice, the sun shines through the door, illuminating the tomb for 17 minutes.

ROCK OF CASHEL (County Tipperary) Once the seat of the Kings of Munster and later given to the church, this group of medieval buildings contains a perfectly preserved round tower, a castle, and a Romanesque chapel. Look for the High Crosses.

TRIM CASTLE (County Meath) Founded by Hugh de Lacy, a Norman knight, this is the largest medieval castle in Ireland. Look for it in the Mel Gibson film *Braveheart*.

Ireland's Thirty-Two

There's in Ulster nine in all
Armagh, Antrim, Donegal
Here's to Cavan and to Derry and Tyrone
To Fermanagh, Monaghan, Down
We'll throw out the puppet's crown
Until Ireland's thirty-two is all our own

Chorus
Here's to old Ireland undivided
To all good Irishmen and true
The North, the South, the East and West
They will be forever blessed
One for all and all for Ireland's thirty-two

Onto Leinster now we go
Dublin, Longford and Wicklow
Through to Carlow, Louth, Kilkenny
and Kildare

68

To Westmeath, to Meath and Leix
Full of nature's beauty scene
While Offaly and Wexford take
    their share

    Chorus

Limerick and the treaty stone
Has in Ireland's history shown
Why Kerry sent O'Connell on
    to Clare
Brilliant Meagher of the sword
Forced the light in Waterford
Rebel Cork and Tipperary do
    and dare

    Chorus

Connacht province has but five
The West's awake and much alive
Sligo, Galway and Roscommon fought the foe
Leitrim out of Shannon's fame
Singing high I proudly name
Of that grand and lovely county of Mayo

69

BAKER BYRNE'S BROWN BREAD

Brown bread is a staple in Ireland, and while my grandmother's father was known as "the baker Byrne" in the teeny-tiny town of Baltinglas, County Wicklow, mysteriously none of his recipes survive. Still, he must have made something just like this.

1 cup all-purpose flour
2 tablespoons sugar
1 teaspoon baking powder
1 teaspoon baking soda
$^1/_2$ teaspoon salt
$1^1/_2$ tablespoons butter, in small pieces
2 cups whole wheat pastry flour
$^1/_4$ cup rolled oats
$1^1/_2$ cups buttermilk
Milk

1. Preheat the oven to 375° F.
2. Mix the all-purpose flour, sugar, baking powder, baking soda, and salt. Work the butter into the mix with your hands, rubbing it through until the mixture resembles coarse crumbs. Stir in the whole wheat pastry flour and oats.
3. Gently stir in the buttermilk. If the mixture is too dry to hold together, add milk 1 teaspoon at a time just until the dough holds together. It should not be sticky.
4. Turn the dough onto a floured board and knead gently five times. Form the dough into a ball. Set on a greased baking sheet and pat into a 7-inch circle. With a floured knife, cut a large X on top.
5. Bake in the center of the oven for about 40 minutes, until well browned. Cool on a rack for 10 minutes. Serve warm or cool with pure Irish butter.

Yield: 1 loaf.

The Fairy Race
by Lady Francesca Speranza Wilde

The *Sidhe*, or spirit race, called also the *Feadh-Ree*, or fairies, are supposed to have been once angels in heaven, who were cast out by Divine command as a punishment for their inordinate pride.

Some fell to earth, and dwelt there, long before man was created, as the first gods of the earth. Others fell into the sea, and they built themselves beautiful fairy palaces of crystal and pearl underneath the waves; but on moonlight nights they often come up on the land, riding their white horses, and they hold revels with their fairy kindred of the earth, who live in the clefts of the hills, and they dance together on the greensward under the ancient trees, and drink nectar from the cups of the flowers, which is the fairy wine . . .

The fairies of the earth are small and beautiful. They

MYTHS & FOLK TALES

The Fairy Race

passionately love music and dancing, and live luxuriously in their palaces under the hills and in the deep mountain caves; and they can obtain all things lovely for their fairy homes, merely by the strength of their magic power. They can also assume all forms, and will never know death until the last day comes, when their doom is to vanish away—to be annihilated for ever. But they are very jealous of the human race who are so tall and strong, and to whom has been promised immortality. And they are often tempted by the beauty of a mortal woman and greatly desire to have her as a wife.

The Fairies

by William Allingham

Up the airy mountain,
  Down the rushy glen,
We daren't go a-hunting
  For fear of little men;
Wee folk, good folk,
  Trooping all together;
Green jacket, red cap,
  And white owl's feather!

Down along the rocky shore
  Some make their home—
They live on crispy pancakes
  Of yellow tide-foam;
Some in the reeds
  Of the black mountain lake,
With frogs for their watch-dogs,
  All night awake.

High on the hill-top
  The old King sits;
He is now so old and grey
  He's nigh lost his wits.
With a bridge of white mist
  Columbkill he crosses,
On his stately journeys
  From Slieveleague to Rosses;
Or going up with music
  On cold starry nights,
To sup with the Queen
  Of the gay Northern Lights.

They stole little Bridget
  For seven years long;
When she came down again
  Her friends were all gone.

They took her lightly back,
    Between the night and morrow;
They thought that she was fast
    asleep,
    But she was dead with sorrow.
They have kept her ever since
    Deep within the lake,
On a bed of flag-leaves,
    Watching till she wake.

By the craggy hill-side,
    Through the mosses bare,
They have planted thorn-trees
    For pleasure here and there.
Is any man so daring
    As dig one up in spite,
He shall find their sharpest thorns
    In his bed at night.

Up the airy mountain,
    Down the rushy glen,
We daren't go a-hunting

For fear of little men;
Wee folk, good folk,
    Trooping all together;
Green jacket, red cap,
    And white owl's feather!

FACTS & FANCY
THE CLÁIRSEACH

Ireland is the only country in the world with a musical instrument as a national symbol. The cláirseach, or Irish harp, comes from the Scottish instrument clársach, which is derived from *clár*, meaning "a board." An ancient instrument, the cláirseach has been found in Irish stone carvings dating to the 10th century and reached its height of popularity in the Middle Ages. (The Brian Boru is the oldest surviving Irish harp, dating back to the late 14th century, and is on permanent display in the library of Trinity College, Dublin.) Not only did harp skills bring prestige, praise, and even monetary gain to those who entertained the medieval cultural elite, but harpist poets and bards were seen as troublemakers and rebels by English colonial powers. Queen Elizabeth I detested harpists so much that she ordered Lord Barrymore to "hang the harpers wherever found and destroy their instruments." Despite such opposition, use of the harp continued as an instrument and a symbol, appearing on Irish coinage in the 16th century by order of Henry VIII as well as on the Irish coat of arms, passports, flags, presidential seals, and the present Irish euro coins. ❧

The Mountains of

Oh, Mary, this London's a wonderful sight,
With people all working by day and by night.
Sure they don't sow potatoes, nor barley, nor wheat,
But there's gangs of them digging for gold in the street.
At least when I asked them that's what I was told,
So I just took a hand at this digging for gold,
But for all that I found there I might as well be
Where the Mountains of Mourne sweep down to the sea.

I believe that when writing a wish you expressed
As to know how the fine ladies in London were dressed,
Well if you'll believe me, when asked to a ball,
They don't wear no top to their dresses at all,
Oh I've seen them meself and you could not in truth,
Say that if they were bound for a ball or a bath.
Don't be starting such fashions, now, Mary McCree,
Where the Mountains of Mourne sweep down to the sea.

I've seen England's king from the top of a bus
And I've never known him, but he means to know us.
And tho' by the Saxon we once were oppressed,

Mourne by Percy French

Still I cheered, God forgive me, I cheered with the rest,
And now that he's visited Erin's green shore
We'll be much better friends than we've been heretofore
When we've got all we want, we're as quiet as can be
Where the Mountains of Mourne sweep down to the sea.

You remember young Peter O'Loughlin, of course,
Well, now he is here at the head of the force.
I met him today, I was crossing the Strand,
And he stopped the whole street with a wave of his hand.
And there we stood talkin' of days that are gone,
While the whole population of London looked on.
But for all these great powers he's wishful like me,
To be back where the dark Mourne sweeps down to the sea.

There's beautiful girls here, oh never you mind,
With beautiful shapes nature never designed,
And lovely complexions all roses and cream,
But let me remark with regard to the same:
That if that those roses you venture to sip,
The colours might all come away on your lip,
So I'll wait for the wild rose that's waiting for me
In the place where the dark Mourne sweeps down to the sea.

The Legend of Finn Mac Cumhal

Finn was the last and greatest leader of the Fianna, the warrior-hunters who served the High King of Ireland in the 3rd century A.D. At his birth, Finn's father Cumhal had been killed in battle by the sons of Morna, and his mother Muirne dared not keep him. She sent him to live in the woods with two women, a druid and a warrior-woman, who raised him in secret, teaching him the arts of war and hunting. When he grew older, he ran away with a troop of poets to hide from his enemies. In this passage Lady Gregory tells of Finn's two great encounters with wisdom during his travels.

And then he said farewell to Crimall, and went on to learn poetry from Finegas, a poet that was living at the Boinn, for the poets thought it was always on the brink of water poetry was revealed to them. And he did not give him his own name, but he took the name of Deimne. Seven years, now, Finegas had stopped at the Boinn, watching the salmon, for it was in the

MYTHS & FOLK TALES

The Legend of Finn Mac Cumhal

prophecy that he would eat the salmon of knowledge that would come there, and that he would have all knowledge after. And when at the last the salmon of knowledge came, he brought it to where Finn was, and bade him to roast it, but he bade him not to eat any of it. And when Finn brought him the salmon after a while he said: "Did you eat any of it at all, boy?" "I did not," said Finn; "but I burned my thumb putting down a blister that rose on the skin, and after that, I put my thumb in my mouth." "What is your name, boy?" said Finegas. "Deimne," said he. "It is not, but it is Finn your name is, and it is to you and not to myself the salmon was given in the prophecy."

MYTHS & FOLK TALES

The Legend of Finn Mac Cumhal

With that he gave Finn the whole of the salmon, and from that time Finn had the knowledge that came from the nuts of the nine hazels of wisdom that grow beside the well that is below the sea.

And besides the wisdom he got then, there was a second wisdom came to him another time, and this is the way it happened. There was a well of the moon belonging to Beag, son of Buan, of the Tuatha de Danaan, and whoever would drink out of it would get wisdom, and after a second drink he would get the gift of foretelling. And the three daughters of Beag, son of Buan, had charge of the well, and they would not part with a vessel of it for anything less than red gold. And one day Finn chanced to be hunting in the rushes near the well, and the three women ran out to hinder him from coming to it, and one of them that had a vessel of water in her hand, threw it at him to stop him, and a share of the water went into his mouth. And from that day out he had all the knowledge that the water of that well could give.

The Meeting of the Waters

by Thomas Moore

There is not in the wide world a valley so sweet
As that vale in whose bosom the bright waters meet;
Oh! the last rays of feeling and life must depart,
Ere the bloom of that valley shall fade from my heart.

Yet it was not that Nature had shed o'er the scene
Her purest of crystal and brightest of green;
'Twas not her soft magic of streamlet or hill,
Oh! no,—it was something more exquisite still.

'Twas that friends, the belov'd of my bosom, were near,
Who made every dear scene of enchantment more dear,
And who felt how the best charms of nature improve,
When we see them reflected from looks that we love.

Sweet vale of Avoca! how calm could I rest
In thy bosom of shade, with the friends I love best,
Where the storms that we feel in this cold world should cease,
And our hearts, like thy waters, be mingled in peace.

THE MATTER WITH IRELAND

BY GEORGE BERNARD SHAW

Irish people are, like most country people, civil and kindly when they are treated with due respect. But anyone who, under the influence of the stage Irishman and the early novels of Lever, treats a tour in Ireland as a lark, and the people as farce actors who may be addressed as Pat and Biddy, will have about as much success as if he were to paint his nose red and interrupt a sermon in Westminster Abbey by addressing music-hall patter to the dean. Also there are certain bustling nuances of manner which are popular in a busy place like England because they save time and ceremony, but which strike an Irishman as too peremptory and too familiar, and are resented accordingly. You need be no more ceremonious in word or gesture than in England; but your attitude had better be the Latin attitude which you have learned in Italy and France, and not the Saxon attitude learned in England and Bavaria. It is as well to know, by the way, that there are no Celts in Ireland and never have been, though there are many Iberians. The only European nation where the typical native is also a typical Celt is Prussia.

As an illustration of the sort of police activity which is peculiar to Ireland, I will give an experience of my own. One evening in the south of Donegal it was

getting dark rapidly, and, after being repeatedly disappointed of finding our desti-
nation round the next corner, as tired people will expect, we had at last grown desperate and settled down to drive another twenty miles as fast as the road would let
us before the light failed altogether.

The result was that we came suddenly round a bend and over a bridge right
into the middle of the tiny town before we supposed our selves to be within five
miles of it. The whole population had assembled in the open for evening gossip,
and we dashed through them at a speed considerably in excess of the ten-mile
limit. They scattered in all directions, and a magnificent
black retriever charged us like a wolf, barking
frantically. My chauffeur, who was driving,
made a perilous swerve and just saved the
dog by a miracle of dexterity. Then we
drew up at the porch of the hotel,
and I looked anxiously back
at the crowd, hoping it did
not include a member of
the R.I.C. Alas, it did, and
he was a stern-faced man
whose deliberate stalk in our

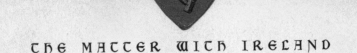

direction could have only one object. The crowd, which had taken our rush with the utmost goodhumor, did not gather to witness our discomfiture as a city crowd would have done. It listened, but pretended not to, as a matter of good breeding. The inspector inspected us up and down until we shrank into mere guilty worms. He then addressed my chauffeur in these memorable words: "What sort of a man are you? Here you come into a village where there's a brute of a dog that has nearly ate two childer, and it is the curse and terror of this countryside, and when you get a square chance of killing him you twist your car out of the way and nearly upset it. What sort of a man are you at all?"

My own opinion is that any Briton who does not need at least a fortnight in Ireland once a year to freshen him up has not really been doing his duty. ●

GEORGE BERNARD SHAW (1856–1950). Free thinker, defender of women's rights, and Irish dramatist, Shaw was born and educated in Dublin but moved to London in the 1870s to begin his career. There his first successes came as music and drama critic before playwriting. A socialist and pacifist, he fought for the lives of the rebels slated for execution after the Easter Rising and befriended IRA leader Michael Collins. A film fanatic, he is the only person to win both the Nobel Prize (for literature in 1925) and an Academy Award (for best screenplay, *Pygmalion*, in 1938).

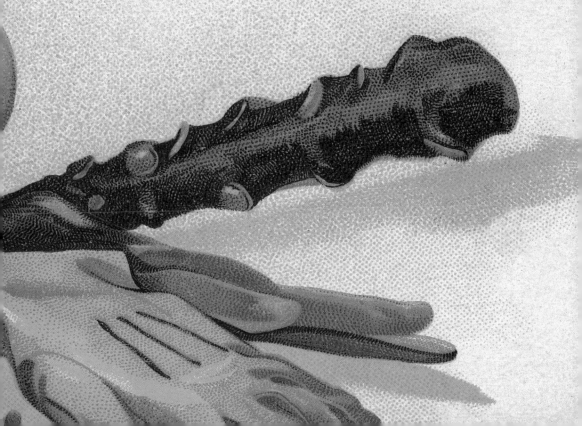

i am not english. i am irish—
which is quite another thing.

—Oscar Fingal O'Flahertie Wills Wilde

If Ever You Go To Dublin Town

by Patrick Kavanagh

If you ever go to Dublin town
In a hundred years or so
Inquire for me in Baggot Street
And what I was like to know.
O he was a queer one,
Fol dol the di do,
He was a queer one
I tell you.

My great-grandmother knew him well,
He asked her to come and call
On him in his flat and she giggled at the thought
Of a young girl's lovely fall.
O he was dangerous
Fol dol the di do
He was dangerous
I tell you.

On Pembroke Road look out for my ghost,
Dishevelled with shoes untied,
Playing through the railings with little children
Whose children have long since died.
O he was a nice man,
Fol dol the di do,
He was a nice man
I tell you.

Go into a pub and listen well
If my voice still echoes there,
Ask the men what their grandsires thought
And tell them to answer fair.
O he was eccentric,
Fol dol the di do,
He was eccentric
I tell you.

He had the knack of making men feel
As small as they really were
Which meant as great as God had made them
But as males they disliked his air.
O he was a proud one,
Fol dol the di do,
He was a proud one
I tell you.

If ever you go to Dublin town
In a hundred years or so
Sniff for my personality,
Is it Vanity's vapour now?
O he was a vain one,
Fol dol the di do,
He was a vain one
I tell you.

94

I saw his name with a hundred others
In a book in the library,
It said he had never fully achieved
His potentiality.
O he was slothful,
Fol dol the di do,
He was slothful
I tell you.

He knew that posterity has no use
For anything but the soul,
The lines that speak the passionate heart,
The spirit that lives alone.
O he was a lone one,
Fol dol the di do
Yet he lived happily
I tell you.

IRISH SODA BREAD

*W*hen my aunt Kay sent me my grandmother's soda bread recipe, there were a lot of directions like "a wee bit of," "to taste," and "you kinda have to . . ." Then I remembered my brother Eddy (the chemical engineer) following my grandmother around her tiny Bronx kitchen, taking notes as she cooked, and asking in complete astonishment, "But don't you know how much, Grandma?" So instead of such Irish vagaries, here's the recipe I use for St. Paddy's Day. It's not Grandma's, but it's really tasty.

3 cups all-purpose flour
1 cup whole wheat pastry flour
3 tablespoons sugar or sucanat
1 tablespoon baking powder
1 teaspoon salt
1 teaspoon baking soda
6 tablespoons butter
2 tablespoons caraway seeds
$1^1/_2$ cups raisins
2 eggs
$1^1/_2$ cups buttermilk

1. Preheat the oven to 350° F. Butter a 2-quart round casserole.
2. Combine the first six ingredients in a large mixing bowl. With your hands, rub in the butter until the mixture resembles coarse crumbs. Stir in the caraway seeds and raisins.
3. In a separate cup, beat the eggs slightly. Remove 1 tablespoon of the beaten egg and set aside. Stir the remaining egg and buttermilk into the flour mixture just until the flour is moist. It should be sticky.

4. Turn the dough onto a well-floured surface and knead 8 to 10 strokes to mix thoroughly. Make the dough into a ball and place it in the casserole. Cut an X into the top and brush on the reserved slightly beaten egg.

5. Bake the bread for 1 hour and 20 minutes, or until a toothpick inserted in the center of the loaf comes out clean. Cool on a rack for 10 minutes, then remove from the casserole and serve steaming hot with loads of butter. Toast the leftovers for breakfast the next day.

Yield: 1 loaf.

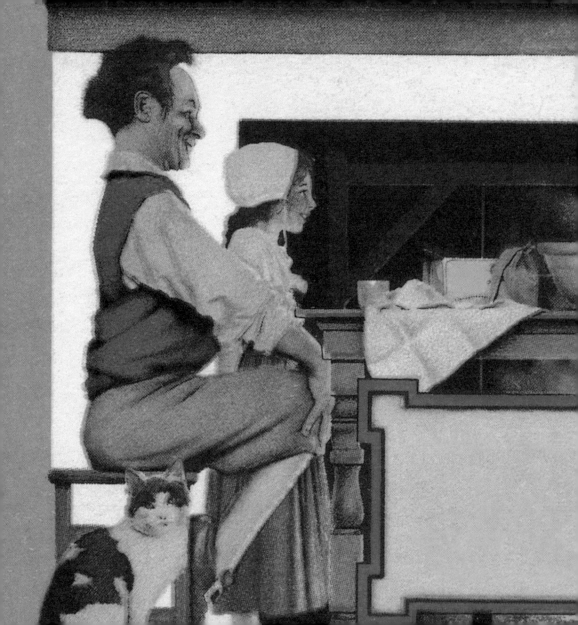

FACTS & FANCY
ANNUAL FESTIVALS

As U2's Bono might say, Irish culture is "alive and kicking," and festivals (also known by the Irish word fleadh) are held throughout the country (mostly in the summer) to celebrate. And while music comes nearly as naturally as breathing to the Irish—and is well represented at festivals—there are also celebrations of dance, theater, poetry, comedy, food, fishing, and even matchmaking. If you miss any of these, a visit to the local pub makes a good substitute, providing plenty of Guinness, gossip, and craic—and maybe even some fiddling!

ANGLING (Fishing, in American)

JUNE: Prosperous 3-Day Festival
(Prosperous, County Kildare) Angle for prizes (and fish) on shore and at sea.

JUNE: Westport Sea Angling Festival
(Westport, County Mayo) Attend the longest-running sea-angling event in Europe.

COMEDY

JUNE: Smithwicks Cat Laugh Festival
(Kilkenny, County Kilkenny; *smithwickscat-laughs.com*) Besides the four days of stand-up, there is the infamous "Ireland v. The Rest of The World" comedians' soccer game.

DRAMA/THEATER

JULY: Earagail Arts Festival (County Donegal; *eaf.ie*) This celebration features two weeks of theater (and some art and music) with venues in more than twenty towns and villages.

SEPTEMBER: Dublin Fringe Festival (Dublin; *fringefest.com*) Off-off (off) Broadway. The Fringe is one of Europe's leading independent, daring and experimental theater fests.

CLAN RALLY

YEAR ROUND: Clan Rallies
(*irishclangatherings.com*) While not
strictly a festival, chances are there's a
gathering of your clan on the Emerald
Isle every few years.

Annual Festivals

SEPTEMBER: **Dublin Theatre Festival** (Dublin; *dublintheatrefestival.com*) For half a century, this festival has been a showcase of Irish drama balanced with the best international theater available.

Food

AUGUST: **Irish Coffee Festival** (Foynes, County Limerick) See who wins the World Irish Coffee Making Championship, and then take a sip or two.

SEPTEMBER: **Galway Oyster Festival** (Galway City, County Galway; *galwayoysterfest.com*) They claim to have Ireland's best, and they go perfectly with a pint of stout. Join the oyster-opening contest if you dare!

OCTOBER: **Kinsale Fine Food Festival** (Kinsale, County Cork) Originally a medieval fishing port, Kinsale is now known as the Culinary Capital of Ireland.

Music

MAY: **Kilkenny Rhythm 'n Roots Festival** (Kilkenny, County Kilkenny) Large venues and small pubs fill with alt-country and roots-based music and its fans.

JUNE: **West Cork Chamber Music Festival** (West Cork, County Cork; *westcorkmusic.ie*) This features lots of strings and the occasional flute.

AUGUST: **Ballyshannon Traditional Music Festival** (Ballyshannon, County Donegal) Once a small town gathering, this traditional festival has become one of Ireland's most popular.

AUGUST: **Fleadh Cheoil na hÉireann** (location varies) The Olympics of traditional Irish song, talk, dance, and drink, where more than 200,000 gather to experience the best the country has to offer.

OCTOBER: **Wexford Festival Opera** (Wexford, County Wexford; *wexfordopera.com*) For more than half a century, opera buffs have come to hear the divas sing.

Traditional

APRIL: **Pan Celtic Festival** (venues vary) The Celtic world—Ireland, Scotland, Brittany,

ANNUAL FESTIVALS

the Isle of Man, Cornwall and Wales—gather to sing, dance, and play games, all in Celtic.

MAY: Fleadh Nua (Ennis, County Clare; *fleadhnua.com*) Enjoy a week of story-telling, céilithe, lectures, film, music and more. Fifty thousand attend.

AUGUST: Puck Fair (Killorglin, County Kerry; *puckfair.ie*) This is one of Ireland's oldest and most traditional fairs, dating back 400 years.

WALKING

JUNE/JULY: Castlebar International Four Days' Walking Festival (Castlebar, County Mayo; *castlebar4days walk.com*) Ramble over bog roads and wild moorland by day; revel in music and dance (if you can) at the pubs by night. "The four days are easy," says Tom Maguire of the Dublin Walking Club, "it's the five nights that would kill you."

TRADITIONAL

SEPTEMBER: Lisdoonvarna Match-making Festival (Lisdoonvarna, County Clare) Fed up with Internet dating? Try Ireland's biggest singles party.

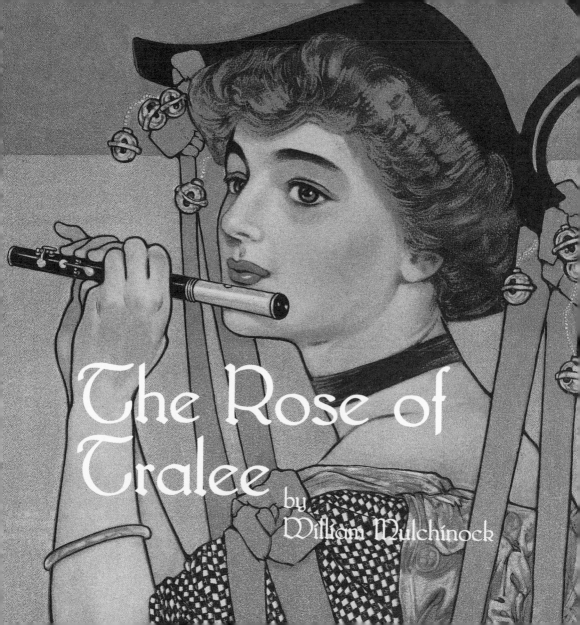

The Rose of Tralee

by
William Mulchinock

The pale moon was rising above the green mountain,
The sun was declining beneath the blue sea,
When I stray'd with my love to the pure
    crystal fountain
That stands in the beautiful vale of Tralee:

Chorus
She was lovely and fair as the rose of the summer
Yet, 'twas not her beauty alone that won me,
Oh, no! 'twas the truth in her eye ever dawning,
That made me love Mary, the Rose of Tralee.

The cool shades of ev'ning their mantle were
    spreading,
And Mary all smiling was list'ning to me,
The moon thro' the valley her pale rays was
    shedding,
When I won the heart of the Rose of Tralee:

Chorus

When anyone asks me about the irish character, i say look at the trees. Maimed, stark and misshapen, but ferociously tenacious.

—Edna O'Brien

A FANATIC HEART

BY EDNA O'BRIEN

I loved my mother, yet I was glad when the time came to go to her mother's house each summer. It was a little house in the mountains and it commanded a fine view of the valley and the great lake below. From the front door, glimpsed through a pair of very old binoculars, one could see the entire Shannon Lake studded with various islands. On a summer's day this was a thrill. I would be put standing on a kitchen chair, while someone held the binoculars, and sometimes I marveled though I could not see at all, as the lenses had not been focused properly. The sunshine made everything better, and though we were not down by the lake, we imagined dipping our feet in it, or seeing people in boats fishing and then stopping to have a picnic. We imagined lake water lapping.

I felt safer in that house. It was different from our house, not so imposing, a cottage really, with no indoor water and no water closet. We went for buckets of water to the well, a different well each summer. These were a source of miracle to me, these deep cold wells, sunk into the ground, in a kitchen garden, or a paddock, or even a long distance away, wells that had been divined since I was last there. There was always a tin scoop nearby so that one could fill the bucket to the very brim. Then of course the full bucket was an occasion of trepidation, because one was supposed not to spill. One often brought the bucket to the very threshold of

A FANATIC HEART

the kitchen and then out of excitement or clumsiness some water would get splashed onto the concrete floor and there would be admonishments, but it was not like the admonishments in our house, it was not calamitous.

My grandfather was old and thin and hoary when I first saw him. His skin was the color of a clay pipe. After the market day he would come home in the pony and trap drunk, and then as soon as he stepped out of the trap he would stagger and fall into a drain or whatever. Then he would roar for help, and his grandson, who was in his twenties, would pick him up, or rather, drag him along the ground and through the house and up the stairs to his feather bed, where he moaned and

groaned. The bedroom was above the kitchen, and in the night we would be below, around the fire, eating warm soda bread and drinking cocoa. There was nothing like it. The fresh bread would only be an hour out of the pot and cut in thick pieces and dolloped with butter and greengage jam. The greengage jam was a present from the postmistress, who gave it in return for the grazing of a bullock. She gave marmalade at a different time of year and a barmbrack at Halloween. He moaned upstairs, but no one was frightened of him, not even his own wife, who chewed and chewed and said, "Bad cess to them that give him the drink." She meant the publicans. She was a minute woman with a minute face and her thin hair was pinned up tightly. Her little face, though old, was like a bud, and when she was young she had been beautiful. There was a photo of her to prove it.

EDNA O'BRIEN (1932–) was born in Twamgraney, County Clare. O'Brien explored the plight of Irish women in a repressed society through bold female characters and often frank sexuality in such works as *The Country Girls*, *The High Road*, and *Time and Tide*, resulting in the banning of several of her works in Ireland.

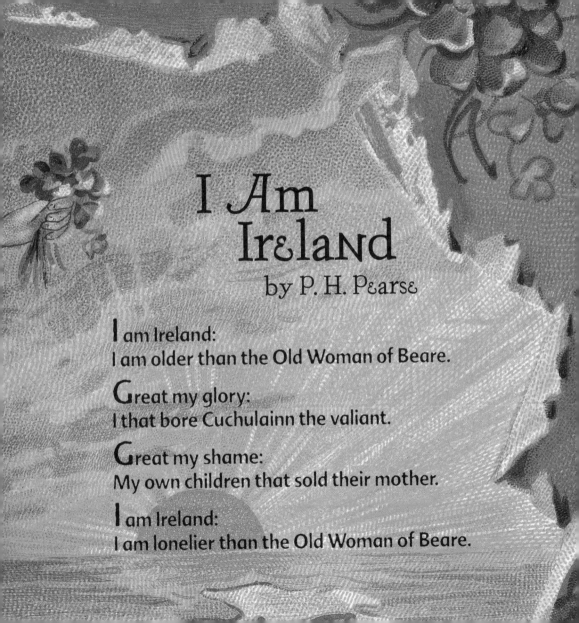

I Am Ireland

by P. H. Pearse

I am Ireland:
I am older than the Old Woman of Beare.

Great my glory:
I that bore Cuchulainn the valiant.

Great my shame:
My own children that sold their mother.

I am Ireland:
I am lonelier than the Old Woman of Beare.

The Famous and the Great*

From scientists and saints to kings and revolutionaries—the Irish and their culture have had a large and lasting impact on the world as a whole. Here are some Irish movers and shakers, past and present.

CONN CÉAD-CATHACH or Conn of the Hundred Battles (110-157): A high king of Ireland known for his audacity in the face of adversity as well as his unconventional surprise-attack techniques, for which he paid dearly.

NIALL NÓIGIALLACH or Niall of the Nine Hostages (d. circa. 450): He consolidated the northern region of Ireland and created a dynasty that kept his descendants high kings of Ireland for 600 years. He also took control of a large portion of Britain, kidnapping Succat-later known as St. Patrick-and bringing him to Ireland.

ST. BRIGID or Mary of the Gael (452-524): One of the three patron saints of Ireland. Legend holds that everything she touched increased in quantity or quality, whether the sheep she tended or food for the poor, but many believe she was an invention of the Catholic Church used to convert pagans to Christianity.

ST. BRENDAN OF KERRY (484-578): Much-disputed legend holds that he voyaged to North America in the sixth century with a group of monks. Petroglyphs of Ogham writings, or alphabetical representations of Gaelic languages, have been found in West Virginia and New Mexico, lending weight to this theory.

---

*Please see page 138 for famous Irish writers.

The Famous and the Great

ST. COLUMBA or Colm Cille (521-597): Of royal blood, he was the outstanding figure among the Gaelic missionary monks who reintroduced Christianity to Scotland during the Dark Ages, as well as a writer, publisher, warrior, scholar, and one of the three patron saints of Ireland.

BRIAN BORU (d. 1014): King of Munster and eventually an extremely powerful high king of Ireland who may have attempted to gain emperor status.

GRACE O'MALLEY or Gráinne Ni Mháille (1530-1603): A famous female pirate, seafarer, trader, and chieftain.

SEAN O'NEILL (1532-c. 1567): He fought the English, Scottish, and Irish over his family's land in Ulster and barred further advancement by the English into this portion of Ireland during the 16th century.

HUGH O'DONNELL (1573-1602): Known as "Red Hugh" of the O'Donnell clan, he led the reclamation of almost all of Ireland until his defeat in 1601 and death by poisoning in 1602.

EDMUND BURKE (1729-1797): Born, raised, and educated in Ireland, Burke was one of the best-known British statesmen and political philosophers of the 18th century, remembered for his vehement opposition to the French Revolution and support for the American Revolution.

RICHARD MARTIN (1754-1834): Founded the Royal Society for the Prevention of Cruelty to Animals.

JAMES HOBAN (1762-1831): Architect, designer, and builder of the White House in Washington, DC.

LORD EDWARD FITZGERALD (1763-1798): This Irish revolutionary's early career was in the army and the Irish House of Commons. Attracted by the French Revolution, he went to Paris, was expelled from the British army for his avowed Republicanism, returned home, and joined the United Irishmen, pledging to assist as commander in chief of their rebel army. He went to Basel to negotiate French aid for the planned Irish uprising, but when he was betrayed by an informer on the eve of the rebellion of 1798, he was arrested and eventually died of wounds sustained at his arrest.

THEOBALD WOLFE TONE (1763-1798): Considered the father of Irish Republicanism and a leader of the revolution of 1798, he helped found United Irishmen. He cut his own throat while incarcerated to avoid giving the British the satisfaction of executing him.

DANIEL O'CONNELL (1775-1847): This statesman and Irish leader in the British House of Commons, known in Ireland as "The Liberator," forced the British to accept the Emancipation Act of 1829, by which Roman Catholics were permitted to sit in Parliament and to hold public office.

ROBERT EMMET (1780-1803): A member of the Society of United Irishmen, he fled British repression at England's declaration of war on France. He later returned to Ireland, helping to organize and participating in the 1803 rebellion, which disintegrated into chaos. Emmet fled into hiding; he was captured, tried, convicted of treason, and hung and beheaded. His remains were secretly buried and never found.

JOHN P. HOLLAND (1841-1914): He played an integral role in the development of the modern submarine.

CHARLES STEWART PARNELL (1846-1891): This Irish Nationalist leader in the late 19th century was elected to Parliament in 1875 and became president of the Irish Land League in 1879. He organized massive land agitation as well as obstruction of parliamentary business.

JAMES CONNOLLY (1868-1916): This labor leader, the first major Marxist leader in Ireland, emigrated to the United States in 1903 and founded the Irish Socialist Federation in New York (1907). He returned to Ireland in 1910 as organizer for the Socialist Party of Ireland and Belfast organizer of the Irish Transport and General Workers Union (1910), serving as acting general secretary of ITGWU, commandant of the Irish Citizen Army (1914), and commandant general of the Dublin Division of the Army of the Republic during the Easter Rising of 1916. Unable to stand due to injuries, he was strapped to a chair to face a firing squad.

ERNEST SHACKLETON (1874-1922): A member of Robert F. Scott's 1901-1904 Antarctic expedition, he sledged partway across the Ross ice shelf. In 1914-1916 his expedition ship Endurance was crushed by drifting pack ice; he and five of his men traveled 800 miles in a whaleboat to South Georgia Island to get aid. Shackleton led four relief expeditions before rescuing his men.

PATRICK PEARSE (1879-1916): A leader of Irish Nationalism, poet, and educator, he was the first president of the provisional government of the Irish Republic and commander in chief of the Irish forces on Easter Monday, 1916, when the 1916 Rising began. After surrendering to the British, he was sent for court-martial and shot in Kilmainham Gaol on 3 May 1916.

MICHAEL COLLINS (1890-1922): A founding member of the Irish Republican Army, he was an instrumental leader in the treaty of 1921 and considered to have helped create the basis for guerrilla warfare.

MONSIGNOR HUGH O'FLAHERTY (1898-1963): An Irish priest in the Vatican who, during World War II, made it possible for more than 6,000 members of the Allied Expeditionary Force to be safely transported to Switzerland so that they could be returned to their military units. He also persuaded churches in Rome to protect many Jewish people by having baptismal certificates made out in their names.

MARY ROBINSON (b. 1944): Not only the first woman president of Ireland, she was, at the time, one of only three female heads of state in the world. Robinson resigned the presidency on 12 September 1997, 11 weeks short of her full seven-year term, to accept the position of United Nations High Commissioner for Human Rights.

MYTHS & FOLK TALES

The Banshee

by Lady Francesca Speranza Wilde

The Banshee is the *spirit of death*, the most weird and awful of all the fairy powers.

But only certain families of historic lineage, or persons gifted with music and song, are attended by this spirit; for music and poetry are fairy gifts, and the possessors of them show kinship to the spirit race—therefore they are watched over by the spirit of life, which is prophecy and inspiration; and by the spirit of doom, which is the revealer of the secrets of death.

Sometimes the Banshee assumes the form of some sweet singing virgin of the family who died young, and has been given the mission by the invisible powers to become the harbinger of coming doom to her mortal kindred. Or she may be seen at night as a shrouded woman, crouched beneath the trees, lamenting with veiled face; or flying past in the moon-

The Banshee

light, crying bitterly: and the cry of thus spirit is mournful beyond all other sounds on earth, and betokens certain death to some member of the family whenever it is heard in the silence of the night . . .

~

There was a gentleman who had a beautiful daughter, strong and healthy, and a splendid horsewoman. She always followed the hounds, and her appearance at the hunt attracted unbounded admiration, as no one rode so well or looked so beautiful.

One evening there was a ball after the hunt, and the young girl moved through the dance with the grace of a fairy queen.

But that same night a voice came close to the father's window, as if the face were laid close to the glass, and he heard a mournful lamentation and a cry; and the words rang out on the air—"In three weeks death; in three weeks the grave—dead—dead—dead!"

The Banshee

Three times the voice came, and three times he heard the words; but though it was bright moonlight, and he looked from the window over all the park, no form was to be seen.

Next day, his daughter showed symptoms of fever, and exactly in three weeks, as the Banshee had prophesied, the beautiful girl lay dead.

The night before her death soft music was heard outside the house, though no word was spoken by the spirit-voice, and the family said the form of a woman crouched beneath a tree, with a mantle covering her head, was distinctly visible. But on approaching, the phantom disappeared, though the soft, low music of the lamentation continued till dawn.

Then the angel of death entered the house with soundless feet, and he breathed upon the beautiful face of the young girl, and she rested in the sleep of the dead, beneath the dark shadows of his wings.

Thus the prophecy of the Banshee came true, according to the time foretold by the spirit-voice.

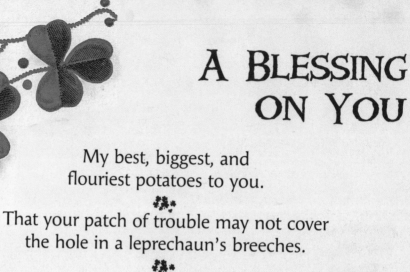

A Blessing on You

My best, biggest, and
flouriest potatoes to you.

That your patch of trouble may not cover
the hole in a leprechaun's breeches.

May you escape the gallows, avoid distress,
and be as healthy as a trout.

May the Good Lord take a
liking to you . . . but not too soon!

Sláinte an bhradáin agat.
(Health of the salmon to you.)

God spare you the years to smoke
your dudeen, drink your cruiskeen,
flourish your alpeen to wallop a spalpeen.

May the wind be always at your back,
especially coming home on Saturday night.

As you slide down the banister of life, may
the splinters never point the wrong way.

May the leprechauns dance over your
bed and bring you sweet dreams.

May you have a gentleman
for a landlord.

Aunt Joan's Colcannon

*T*rust me, this mashed-potato-plus dish does not require precision. When Aunt Joan gave me this recipe, I continually pressed her with questions like, "Well, how much water?" and "What do you mean, 'not too much'?" and "Can you give me any idea how long will it take?" It doesn't matter. Colcannon is easy to make, and while it remains practically unknown, it is surprisingly tasty. Everyone always likes it.

1 head cabbage (a nice-size one)
5–6 potatoes (the kind that are best boiled: new potatoes, round red, white, or long whites), peeled (as Aunt Joan instructed) or unpeeled (as I like them)
1 bunch scallions
Lots of butter (at least a stick)
Salt and pepper

1. Wash and cut the cabbage and potatoes into chunks. Wash and chop the scallions.
2. Put all into a large pot, add about 1 inch of water ("not too much, but watch it"), and boil.
3. When the potatoes are fork-tender (check at 20 minutes and then every 5 minutes), remove from the heat and mash. Add butter, salt, and pepper to taste.
4. Serve in a bowl, topped with more butter and freshly ground pepper.

Yield: 4–6 servings.

FACTS & FANCY
THE SHILLELAGH

The shillelagh (pronounced *shil-LAY-lee*) is a wooden stick with a large knob on the end and is traditionally used for fighting. It is named after the Shillelagh Forest in County Wicklow, where massive oak trees were once harvested and used to make the canes. The typically black patina of the shillelagh is achieved by burying the stick in a pile of manure or smearing it with butter, then placing it in a chimney to cure. The "smearing" technique keeps the wood from cracking.

If the knob end of the shillelagh is hollowed out and filled with molten lead (for extra bang), it is called a "loaded stick." The stick is held toward the lower middle and snapped out with the wrist, not swung.

Fights using the shillelagh (also known by the Irish word *bata*) were often between feuding families or political groups gathered at social events like a fair or even a wake. Sometimes, however, fights were a sporting event or even just for the fun of it.

In modern times the shillelagh is used by the *X-Men* comic book villain Black Tom Cassidy (an Irish citizen and frequent partner of fellow X-Man Juggernaut). It helps project the blasts of force or heat of his superhuman power. ✳

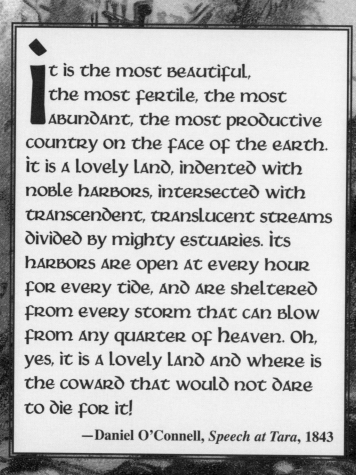

It is the most beautiful, the most fertile, the most abundant, the most productive country on the face of the earth. It is a lovely land, indented with noble harbors, intersected with transcendent, translucent streams divided by mighty estuaries. Its harbors are open at every hour for every tide, and are sheltered from every storm that can blow from any quarter of heaven. Oh, yes, it is a lovely land and where is the coward that would not dare to die for it!

—Daniel O'Connell, *Speech at Tara*, 1843

"DO YOU THINK SHOULD HE HAVE GONE OVER?"

BY JAN MORRIS

I drove along the coast to Howth, and then the Joyceness of Dublin, the Yeatsness, the pubness, the tramness, the Liffeyness, the Behanness, in short the stock Dublinness of the place seemed to hang like vapour over the distant city. It was one of those Irish evenings, when the points of the compass seem to have been confused, and their climates with them. A bitter east wind swayed the palm trees along the promenade, a quick northern air sharpened that slightly Oriental languor, that Celtic *dolce far niente*, which habitually blurs the intentions of Dublin. Over the water the city lay brownish below the Wicklow Mountains, encrusted it seemed with some tangible patina of legend and literature, and fragrant of course with its own *vin du pays*, Guinness.

This is everyone's Dublin, right or wrong, and if it is partly myth, it is substance too. There is no such thing as a stage Dubliner: the characters of this city, even at their most theatrical, are true and earnest in their kind, and Dublin too, even today, lives up to itself without pretense. Are there any urchins like Dublin urchins, grubby as sin and bouncy as ping-pong ball? Are there any markets like Dublin markets, sprawling all over the city streets like gypsy jumble sales? Are there any

buses so evocative as Dublin buses lurching in dim-lit parade towards Glasnevin?

Certainly there are few more boisterous streets on earth than O'Connell Street on a Saturday night, when a salt wind gusts up from the sea, making the girls giggle and the young men clown about, driving the Dublin litter helter-skelter here and there, and eddying the smells of beer, chips and hot-dogs all among the back streets. And there is no café more tumultuous than Bewley's Oriental Café in Grafton Street, with its mountains of buns on every table, with its children draped over floors and chairs, with its harassed waitresses scribbling, its tea-urns hissing, its stained glass and its tiled floors, its old clock beside the door, the high babel of its Dublin chatter and its haughty Dublin ladies, all hats and arched eyebrows, smoking their cigarettes loftily through it all.

It is an all too familiar rhythm, but it beats unmistakably still, hilariously and pathetically, and makes of Dublin one of the most truly exotic cities in the world. ●

JAN MORRIS (1926–), born in Somerset, England, began her writing life as a foreign correspondent for the London *Times*, as a travel writer, as the author of the lauded profile of the progress of the British Empire, *Pax Britannica*, and as a man. James Humphrey Morris underwent sexual reassignment surgery and in 1974 published *Conundrum* documenting her dramatic experiences. Morris's writing style noticeably changed following her transformation, exhibiting what she calls "changed sensibilities," with "a softer prose style, perhaps of softer judgments."

Mairi's Wedding

Over hillways up and down
Myrtle green and bracken brown,
Past the sheilings through the town
All for sake of Mairi.

Chorus
Step we gaily, on we go
Heel for heel and toe for toe,
Arm in arm and row on row
All for Mairi's wedding.

Red her cheeks as rowans are
Bright her eyes as any star,
Fairest o' them all by far
Is our darlin' Mairi.

Chorus

Plenty herring, plenty meal
Plenty peat to fill her creel,
Plenty bonny bairns as weel
That's the toast for Mairi.

Chorus

by
Hugh Robertson

134

Bring home the poet, laurel-crowned,
Lay him to rest in Irish ground;
Make him a grave near Sligo Bay,
At fair Drumcliffe or Knocknarea,
For near his mother's kindred dwelt,
And at Drumcliffe his fathers knelt,
And all about in beauty's haze,
The print of proud, heroic days,
With wind and wave in druid hymn
To chant for aye his requiem.
And he'll have mourners at his bier,
The fairy hosts who hold him dear,
And Father Gilligan, he'll be there,
The martial Maeve and Deirdre fair,
And lads he knew in town and glen,
The fisher folk and sailor men;
The Dooney fiddler and the throng
He made immortal with his song;
And proud in grief his rightful queen,
Ni Houlihan, the brave Kathleen.
Bring home the poet, let him rest
In the old land he loved the best.

Bring Home the Poet

by Patrick MacDonough

FACTS & FANCY
THE IRISH SCRIBE

Irish writers like to provoke. They are not about telling lovely fairy stories with happy endings. Sometimes they're not even about stories at all (read or watch Beckett). What makes Irish writers interesting is that, even if you're not quite sure what they are saying, by the end you notice that you have been poked or prodded—sometimes uncomfortably so— often with a good dose of wit. From political satire (like Jonathan Swift's *Gulliver's Travels*) to religious "critique" like Brendan Behan's *Borstal Boy*, provocation seems somehow bred into the Irish. Even the more mild-mannered George Bernard Shaw had a go: "Christianity might be a good thing if anyone ever tried it."

And when the Irish writer isn't poking at your brain, then he is almost certainly making you cry (Brian Friel's *Dancing at Lughnasa*), or laugh (the plays of Oscar Wilde), or even riot. When Synge's *The Playboy of the Western World* was first staged, one theatergoer described it as "a vile and inhuman story told in the foulest language we have ever listened to from a public platform." Riots ensued; world fame followed.

As for Joyce—the most famous of Irish writers—while *The Dubliners* may be a tough read, his innovative style had a profound effect on 20th-century literature. That said, he never won an Oscar like George Bernard Shaw (Best Screenplay, 1938, for *Pygmalion*).

CLASSIC SCRIBES

SAMUEL BECKETT *Molloy; Malone Dies; Waiting for Godot; The Unnamable; Endgame; Krapp's Last Tape*

BRENDAN BEHAN *The Quare Fellow; Borstal Boy; The Big House; The Hostage*

JAMES JOYCE *Dubliners; Portrait of the Artist as a Young Man; Ulysses; Finnegans Wake; The Cat and the Devil*

FLANN O'BRIEN *At Swim-Two-Birds; The Third Policeman; The Best of Myles; Further Cuttings from Cruiskeen Lawn*

GEORGE BERNARD SHAW *Mrs. Warren's Profession; Major Barbara; Androcles and the Lion; Pygmalion*

JONATHAN SWIFT *A Tale of a Tub; Gulliver's Travels; A Modest Proposal; The Journal to Stella; Arguments Against Abolishing Christianity; Drapier's Letters*

JOHN MILLINGTON SYNGE *Riders to the Sea; The Aran Islands; The Playboy of the Western World; The Tinker's Wedding*

OSCAR WILDE *The Picture of Dorian Gray; Salome; The House of Pomegranates; An Ideal Husband; The Importance of Being Earnest*

WILLIAM BUTLER YEATS *The Celtic Twilight; Cuchulan's Fight with the Sea; A Faery Song; Old Age of Queen Maeve; Sailing to Byzantium; Cathleen Ni Houlihan; The Second Coming; Leda and the Swan; Among School Children; Irish Fairy Tales*

UP-AND-COMERS

RODDY DOYLE *The Commitments; The Snapper; The Van; Paddy Clarke Ha Ha Ha; A Star Called Henry; Oh, Play That Thing!*

BRIAN FRIEL *The Saucer of Larks; The Communication Cord; Making History; Dancing at Lughnasa; The Home Place*

SEAMUS HEANEY *Death of a Naturalist; Door into the Dark; Field Work; The Cure at Troy; District and Circle*

PATRICK MCCABE *The Butcher Boy; The Dead School; Breakfast on Pluto; Emerald Gems of Ireland; Call Me the Breeze*

FRANK MCCOURT *A Couple of Blaguards; Angela's Ashes; 'Tis; Teacher Man*

MARTIN MCDONAGH *Beauty Queen of Leenane; A Skull in Connemara; The Lonesome West; The Pillowman; The Lieutenant of Inishmore*

SERPENT LA

K

GAP OF DUNLOE,
RNEY.

The Bull of Cuailgne

The Bull of Cuailgne is the central story of the Ulster Cycle of Irish mythology, in which Queen Maeve pits the forces of Connaught against those of Ulster, as well as dear friends Cuchulain and Ferdiadin, in a fierce battle to the death—all over the jealousy of the King's wealth. In this passage Lady Gregory portrays the genesis of the battle in the argument between Queen Maeve and King Ailell.

And if I took the daughter of the chief king of Ireland for my wife, it was because I thought she was a fitting wife for me." "You know well," said Maeve, "the riches that belong to me are greater than the riches that belong to you." "That is a wonder to me," said Ailell, "for there is no one in Ireland has a better store of jewels and riches and treasure than myself, and you know well there is not."

"Let our goods and our riches be put beside one another, and let a value be put on them," said Maeve, "and you will know which of us owns most." "I am content to do that," said Ailell.

The Bull of Cuailgne

With that, orders were given to their people to bring out their goods and to count them, and to put a value on them. They did so, and the first things they brought out were their drinking vessels, their vats, their iron vessels, and all the things belonging to their households, and they were found to be equal. Then their rings were brought out, and their bracelets and chains and brooches, their clothing of crimson and blue and black and green and yellow and saffron and speckled silks, and these were found to be equal. Then their great flocks of sheep were driven from the green plains of the open country and were counted, and they were found to be equal; and if there was a ram among Maeve's flocks that was the equal of a serving-maid in value, Ailell had one that was as good. And their horses were brought in from the meadows, and their herds of swine out of the woods and the valleys, and they were equal one to another. And the last thing that was done was to bring in the herds of cattle from the forest and the wild places of the province, and when they were put beside one another they were found to be equal, but for one thing only. It happened a bull had been calved in Maeve's herd, and his name was Fionnbanach, the White-horned. But he would not stop in Maeve's herds,

The Bull of Cuailgne

for he did not think it fitting to be under the rule of a woman, and he had gone into Ailell's herds and stopped there; and now he was the best bull in the whole province of Connaught. And when Maeve saw him, and knew he was better than any bull of her own, there was great vexation on her, and it was as bad to her as if she did not own one head of cattle at all. So she called Mac Roth, the herald, to her, and bade him to find out where there was a bull as good as the White-horned to be got in any province of the provinces of Ireland.

"I myself know that well," said Mac Roth, "for there is a bull that is twice as good as himself at the house of Daire, son of Fachtna, in the district of Cuailgne, and that is Donn Cuailgne, the Brown Bull of Cuailgne." "Rise up, then," said Maeve, "and make no delay, but go to Daire from me, and ask the loan of that bull for a year, and I will return him at the end of the year, and fifty heifers along with him, as fee for the loan."

~

On the morning of the morrow the messengers rose up and went into the house where Daire was. "Show us now," they said, "the place where the bull is." "I will not indeed," said Daire; "but if it was a habit with me," he

The Bull of Cuailgne

said, "to do treachery to messengers or to travellers or to men on their road, not one of you would go back alive to Cruachan." "What reason have you for this change?" said Mac Roth. "I have a good reason for it, for you were saying last night that if I did not give the bull willingly, I would be forced to give it against my will by Ailell and by Maeve and by Fergus." "If that was said, it was the talk of common messengers, and they after eating and drinking," said Mac Roth, "and it is not fitting for you to take notice of a thing like that."

"It may be so" said Daire; "but for all that, he said "I will not give the bull this time."

They went back then to Cruachan, and Maeve asked news of them, and Mac Roth told her the whole story, how Daire gave them the promise of the bull at first, and refused it afterwards. "What was the reason of that?" she asked. And when it was told her she said: "This riddle is not hard to guess; they did not intend to let us get the bull at all; but now we will take him from them by force," she said.

And this was the cause of the great war for the Brown Bull of Cuailgne.

Cashel of Munster

by Samuel Ferguson

I'd wed you without herds, without money, or rich array,
And I'd wed you on a dewy morning at day-dawn grey;
My bitter woe it is, love, that we are not far away
In Cashel town, though the bare deal board were our marriage bed
  this day!

Oh, fair maid, remember the green hillside,
Remember how I hunted about the valleys wide;
Time now has worn me; my locks are turned to grey,
The year is scarce and I am poor, but send me not, love, away!

Oh, deem not my blood is of base strain, my girl,
Oh, deem not my birth was as the birth of the churl;
Marry me, and prove me, and say soon you will,
That noble blood is written on my right side still!

My purse holds no red gold, no coin
    of the silver white,
No herds are mine to drive through
    the long twilight!
But the pretty girl that would
    take me, all bare though
    I be and lone,
Oh, I'd take her with me kindly
    to the county Tyrone.

Oh, my girl, I can see 'tis in
    trouble you are,
And, oh, my girl, I see 'tis your people's
    reproach you bear:
'I am a girl in trouble for his sake with whom I fly,
And, oh, may no other maiden know such
    reproach as I!'

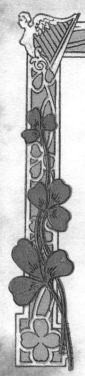

IRISH STEW

*T*he first time my niece Alannah came from Ireland to visit me in New York, she was eight months old. She was not quite on solid food yet, but she brought her parents with her, and they were. So when they arrived—on a gray and blustery November day—I had this hearty Irish stew on the stove. Robbie, Alannah's Dubliner da, had it with Guinness, naturally, while her ma, my sister Jeanne, thought it went perfectly with a full-bodied Burgundy. Either way, nothing says céad míle fáilte *like a bowl of savory Irish stew after a long journey.*

4 tablespoons cooking oil
2 pounds rack or shoulder of lamb, cut into 1-inch cubes
Salt and freshly ground pepper
3 onions, chopped
2 leeks, washed and chopped
2 celery stalks, cut into $^1/_2$-inch pieces
3 potatoes, cut into 1-inch cubes
2 carrots, chopped
3 cloves garlic, minced
2 tablespoons all-purpose flour
2 cups lamb stock (or cold water, red wine, stout, or even beef stock, or any combination of these)
1 10-ounce package frozen peas
1 tablespoon chopped parsley
1 tablespoon chopped fresh thyme
1 small sprig rosemary

1. Heat the oil in large pot or Dutch oven over medium-high heat. Sprinkle the meat with salt and pepper and place in the pot, sautéing until brown on all sides,

about 5 minutes. Using a slotted spoon, remove the meat.

2. Reduce the heat to medium and add the onions, leeks, celery, potatoes, carrots, and garlic to the oil and drippings, stirring for about 2 minutes.

3. Add the flour, stirring constantly for 1 minute, then stir in the stock (or wine, water, what have you), peas, parsley, thyme, and rosemary. Return the lamb to the pot. Bring the stew to a boil, then reduce the heat and cover. Simmer for about 1½ to 2 hours, until the meat is tender.

Yield: 4–6 servings.

Serve with brown bread (page 71) and your choice of stout or wine.

FACTS & FANCY
ST. PATRICK'S DAY

Saint Patrick's Day, a religious feast, was first celebrated—quietly—in Ireland around 500 years after the saint's death (which is thought to be March 17, 460, 461, or maybe 493). In 1903, it became a public holiday in Ireland, and pubs were ordered by law to remain closed. (That law was abolished in the 1970s.)

The earliest celebration in America is thought to be a parade held in Boston in 1737. Twenty-five years later, a group of Irish soldiers serving in the British military brought the spirit of the Irish to New York with a small march in lower Manhattan, and the party has not stopped growing since. That same parade continues in New York today and it ranks number one worldwide in attendance (around 2 million in 2006). But the celebrating hardly stops there. From Dublin to Tokyo, Saint Patrick's Day is celebrated in more countries than any other national holiday, proving that everyone is—at least a little bit—Irish on March 17.

DID YOU KNOW?

Guinness has lobbied the Canadian government to make Saint Patrick's Day a national holiday.

In the U.K., punters compete for a "Guinness Hat," the prize for consuming great quantities of the stout, on March 17.

Former New York mayor Ed Koch once dubbed himself "Ed O'Koch" for the day.

Chicago dyes its rivers green on St. Patrick's Day.

Savannah, Georgia (home to the world's second-largest parade) dyes its fountains green on St. Patrick's Day.

Green was thought to be unlucky in Ireland because it was the favorite color of the "Good People" (fairies) who were likely to steal children who wore too much of it.

A Donegal Fairy

by Letitia Maclintock

Ay, it's a bad thing to displeasure the gentry, sure enough — they can be unfriendly if they're angered, an' they can be the very best o' gude neighbors if they're treated kindly.

My mother's sister was her lone in the house one day, wi' a' big pot o' water boiling on the fire, and ane o' the wee folk fell down the chimney, and slipped wi' his leg in the hot water.

He let a terrible squeal out o' him, an' in a minute the house was full o' wee crathurs pulling him out o' the pot, an' carrying him across the floor.

"Did she scald you?" my aunt heard them saying to him.

"Na, na, it was mysel' scalded my ainsel'," quoth the wee fellow.

"A weel, a weel," says they. "If it was your ainsel' scalded yoursel', we'll say nothing, but if she had scalded you, we'd ha' made her pay."

A Little Cloud

by James Joyce

Eight years before he had seen his friend off at the North Wall and wished him godspeed. Gallaher had got on. You could tell that at once by his traveled air, his well-cut tweed suit, and fearless accent. Few fellows had talents like his and fewer still could remain unspoiled by such success. Gallaher's heart was in the right place and he had deserved to win. It was something to have a friend like that.

Little Chandler's thoughts ever since lunchtime had been of his meeting with Gallaher, of Gallaher's invitation and of the great city London where Gallaher lived. He was called Little Chandler because, though he was but slightly under the average stature, he gave one the idea of being a little man. His hands were white and small, his frame was fragile, his voice was quiet and his manners were refined. He took the greatest care of his fair silken hair and moustache and used perfume discreetly on his handkerchief. The half-moons of his nails were perfect and when he smiled you caught a glimpse of a row of childish white teeth.

As he sat at his desk in the King's Inns he thought what changes those eight years had brought. The friend whom he had known under a shabby and necessitous guise had become a brilliant figure on the London Press. He turned often from his tiresome writing to gaze out of the office window. The glow of a late autumn

sunset covered the grass plots and walks. It cast a shower of kindly golden dust on the untidy nurses and decrepit old men who drowsed on the benches; it flickered upon all the moving figures—on the children who ran screaming along the gravel paths and on everyone who passed through the gardens. He watched the scene and thought of life; and (as always happened when he thought of life) he became sad. A gentle melancholy took possession of him. He felt how useless it was to struggle against fortune, this being the burden of wisdom which the ages had bequeathed to him.

He remembered the books of poetry upon his shelves at home. He had bought them in his bachelor days and many an evening, as he sat in the little room off the hall, he had been tempted to take one down from the bookshelf and read out something to his wife. But shyness had always held him back; and so the books had remained on their shelves. At times he repeated lines to himself and this consoled him.

When his hour had struck he stood up and took leave of his desk and of his fellow-clerks punctiliously. He emerged from under the feudal arch of the King's Inns, a neat modest figure, and walked swiftly down Henrietta Street. The golden sunset was waning and the air had grown sharp. A horde of grimy children populated the street. They stood or ran in the roadway or crawled up the steps before the gaping doors or squatted like mice upon the thresholds. Little Chandler gave them no thought. He picked his way deftly through all that minute vermin-like life

Four Courts, Dublin

and under the shadow of the gaunt spectral mansions in which the old nobility of Dublin had roistered. No memory of the past touched him, for his mind was full of a present joy.

He had never been in Corless's but he knew the value of the name. He knew that people went there after the theatre to eat oysters and drink liqueurs; and he had heard that the waiters there spoke French and German. Walking swiftly by at night he had seen cabs drawn up before the door and richly dressed ladies, escorted by cavaliers, alight and enter quickly. They wore noisy dresses and many wraps. Their faces were powdered and they caught up their dresses, when they touched earth, like alarmed Atalantas. He had always passed without turning his head to look. It was his habit to walk swiftly in the street even by day and whenever he found himself in the city late at night he hurried on his way apprehensively and excitedly. Sometimes, however, he courted the causes of his fear. He chose to darkest and narrowest streets and, as he walked boldly forward, the silence that was spread about his footsteps troubled him, the wandering, silent figures troubled him; and at times a sound of low fugitive laughter made him tremble like a leaf.

He turned to the right towards Capel Street. Ignatius Gallaher on the London Press! Who would have thought it possible eight years before? Still, now that he reviewed the past, Little Chandler could remember many signs of future greatness in his friend. People used to say that Ignatius Gallaher was wild. Of course, he did mix with a rakish set of fellows at that time, drank freely and borrowed money on

A LITTLE CLOUD

all sides. In the end he had got mixed up in some shady affair, some money trans-action: at least, that was one version of his flight. But nobody denied him talent. There was always a certain . . . something in Ignatius Gallaher that impressed you in spite of yourself. Even when he was out at elbows and at his wits' end for money he kept up a bold face. Little Chandler remembered (and the remembrance brought a slight flush of pride to his cheek) one of Ignatius Gallaher's sayings when he was in a tight corner:

"Half time now, boys," he used to say lightheartedly. "Where's my consider-ing cap?"

That was Ignatius Gallaher all out; and, damn it, you couldn't but admire him for it.

Little Chandler quickened his pace. For the first time in his life he felt himself superior to the people he passed. For the first time his soul revolted against the dull inelegance of Capel Street. There was no doubt about it: if you wanted to succeed you had to go away. You could do nothing in Dublin. As he crossed Grattan Bridge he looked down the river towards the lower quays and pitied the poor stunted houses. They seemed to him a band of tramps, huddled together along the river banks, their old coats covered with dust and soot, stupefied by the panorama of sunset and waiting for the first chill of night to bid them arise, shake themselves and begone. He wondered whether he could write a poem to express his idea. Perhaps Gallaher might be able to get it into some London paper for him. Could

he write something original? He was not sure what idea he wished to express but the thought that a poetic moment had touched him took life within him like an infant hope. He stepped onward bravely.

Every step brought him nearer to London, farther from his own sober inartistic life. A light began to tremble on the horizon of his mind. He was not so old—thirty-two. His temperament might be said to be just at the point of maturity. There were so many different moods and impressions that he wished to express in verse. He felt them within him. He tried to weigh his soul to see if it was a poet's soul. Melancholy was the dominant note of his temperament, he thought, but it was a melancholy tempered by recurrences of faith and resignation and simple joy. If he could give expression to it in a book of poems perhaps men would listen. He would never be popular: he saw that. He could not sway the crowd but he might appeal to a little circle of kindred minds. The English critics, perhaps, would recognize him as one of the Celtic school by reason

160

of the melancholy tone of his poems; besides that, he would put in allusions. He began to invent sentences and phrases from the notice which his book would get. *"Mr. Chandler has the gift of easy and graceful verse."* . . . *"A wistful sadness pervades these poems."* . . . *"The Celtic note."* It was a pity his name was not more Irish-looking. Perhaps it would be better to insert his mother's name before the surname: Thomas Malone Chandler, or better still: T. Malone Chandler. He would speak to Gallaher about it. ●

JAMES JOYCE (1882–1941). This most Irish of writers lived almost two-thirds of his life abroad. Born into wealth in suburban Dublin, the Joyces swiftly went from riches to rags as the family increased in size—James being the eldest of 10 surviving children. After graduating from University College Dublin in 1903, he met Nora Barnacle—who bore his children and 27 years later married him—left Ireland to bounce among Zurich, Trieste, Rome, and Paris with the occasional trip back to Ireland, and wrote his first story collection, *Dubliners*, followed by such lauded works as *Portrait of the Artist as a Young Man* and *Ulysses*. Although his themes focused on the common man, his stream-of-consciousness technique and philosophic undertones infused his work with great depth. T. S. Eliot called Joyce's experimental prose "anti-style," yet it had a great influence on modern literature.

FACTS & FANCY
BLOOMSDAY

June 16, 1904, is the day that James Joyce's entire novel *Ulysses* takes place, and so it has become a day Joyceans celebrate around the world. It is also the day that Joyce had his first date with Nora Barnacle, the woman who—27 tempestuous years and two children later—became his wife. The "Bloom" in Bloomsday comes from one of the central characters, Leopold Bloom, an ordinary 38-year-old Jewish advertising agent and Dubliner whom the novel follows for about 18 hours as he wanders through Dublin. Leopold's odyssey is a clear parallel to the ancient Grecian Odysseus's trip, but a little more concrete. It was written with real places and real people in mind; therefore, Dubliners celebrate by dressing as characters from the book and following Leopold's route through the city. Some places are now gone—Bloom's house at 7 Eccles Street, for example (although the front door is at the Joyce Center)—but you can still wander into Davy Byrnes's pub on Duke Street for a gorgonzola sandwich with mustard and a glass of Burgundy wine, exactly as the fictional Leopold Bloom did over a century ago. Along the way, you will likely encounter readings, reenactments, and all kinds of literary lunacy limited only by the Irish imagination.

> *I want to give a picture of Dublin so complete that if the city one day suddenly disappeared from the earth it could be reconstructed out of my book.*
>
> —JAMES JOYCE

However you choose to celebrate, most find that lifting a pint or two is much easier than lifting the actual book (which can run as long as 1000 pages). ❧

Cycling to Dublin

by Robert Greacen

604

Pulling the dead sun's weight through County Meath,
We cycled through the knotted glass of afternoon,
Aware of the bright fog in the narrow slot of breath,
And the cycles' rhyming, coughing croon.

"O hurry to Dublin, to Dublin's fair city,
Where colleens, fair colleens are ever so pretty,
O linger no longer in lumbering langour,
Gallop the miles, the straight-backed miles without number."

We were the Northmen, hard with hoarded words on tongue,
Driven down by home disgust to the broad lands and rich talk,
To the country of poets and pubs and cow-dung
Spouting and sprouting from every stalk. . . .

"O hurry to Dublin, to Dublin's fair city,
Where colleens, fair colleens are ever so pretty,
O linger no longer in lumbering langour,
Gallop the miles, the straight-backed miles without number."

The Children of Lir

Bodb Dearg was elected king of the Tuatha de Danaan, a mystical race of heroes and magicians, much to the displeasure of Lir. To appease Lir, Bodb Dearg gave him one of his daughters as wife, the beautiful and pure-hearted Aobh. Aobh bore Lir four children — daughter Fionnuala, son Aodh, and twin sons Fiachra and Conn, but died at the birth of the twins. Aobh's death weighed heavily on Lir, but he took to wife another of Bodb Dearg's daughters, Aoife, in order to provide maternal comfort to his young children. Lir's children were his joy and delight and Aoife soon noticed the attention and love Lir lavished on them. In a fit of jealousy, Aoife turned the children into swans and cursed them that they would wander the waters of Ireland for 900 years. In this passage by Lady Gregory, the sorrowful Lir finds his cursed children.

I
t is downhearted and sorrowful Lir was at that news, for he understood well it was Aoife had destroyed or made an end of his children. And early in the morning of the morrow his horses were caught, and he set out on the road to the south-west. And when he was as far as the shore of Loch Dairbhreach, the four children saw the horses coming towards them, and it is what Fionnuala said:
"A welcome to the troop of horses I see coming near to the lake; the people

The Children of Lir

they are bringing are strong, there is sadness on them; it is us they are following, it is for us they are looking; let us move over to the shore, Aodh, Fiachra,
and comely Conn. Those that are coming can be no others in the world but
only Lir and his household."

Then Lir came to the edge of the lake, and he took notice of the swans having the voice of living people, and he asked them why was it they had that voice.

"I will tell you that, Lir," said Fionnuala. "We are your own four children,
that are after being destroyed by your wife, and by the sister of our own
mother, through the dint of her jealousy." "Is there any way to put you into
your own shapes again?" said Lir. "There is no way," said Fionnuala, "for all
the men of the world could not help us till we have gone through our time,
and that will not be," she said, "till the end of nine hundred years."

When Lir and his people heard that, they gave out three great heavy
shouts of grief and sorrow and crying.

"Is there a mind with you," said Lir, "to come to us on the land, since you
have your own sense and your memory yet?" "We have not the power," said
Fionnuala, "to live with any person at all from this time; but we have our own
language, the Irish, and we have the power to sing sweet music, and it is
enough to satisfy the whole race of men to be listening to that music. And let
you stop here tonight," she said, "and we will be making music for you."

The Children of Lir

So Lir and his people stopped there listening to the music of the swans, and they slept there quietly that night. And Lir rose up early on the morning of the morrow and he made this complaint:—

"It is time to go from this place. I do not sleep though I am in my lying down. To be parted from my dear children, it is that is tormenting my heart.

"It is a bad net I put over you, bringing Aoife, daughter of Oilell of Aran, to the house. I would never have followed that advice if I had known what it would bring upon me.

"O Fionnuala, and comely Conn, O Aodh, O Fiachra of the beautiful arms; it is not ready I am to go away from you, from the border of the harbor where you are."

Then Lir went on to the palace of Bodb Dearg, and there was a welcome before him there; and he got a reproach from Bodb Dearg for not bringing his children along with him. "My grief!" said Lir. "It is not I that would not bring my children along with me; it was Aoife there beyond, your own foster-child and the sister of their mother, that put them in the shape of four white swans on Loch Dairbhreach, in the sight of the whole of the men of Ireland; but they have their sense with them yet, and their reason, and their voice, and their Irish."

Bodb Dearg gave a great start when he heard that, and he knew what Lir

The Children of Lir

said was true, and he gave a very sharp reproach to Aoife, and he said: "This treachery will be worse for yourself in the end, Aoife, than to the children of Lir. And what shape would you yourself think worst of being in?" he said.

"I would think worst of being a witch of the air," she said. "It is into that shape I will put you now," said Bodb. And with that he struck her with a Druid wand, and she was turned into a witch of the air there and then, and she went away on the wind in that shape, and she is in it yet, and will be in it to the end of life and time.

As to Bodb Dearg and the Tuatha de Danaan they came to the shore of Loch Dairbhreach, and they made their camp there to be listening to the music of the swans.

And the Sons of the Gael used to be coming no less than the Men of Dea to hear them from every part of Ireland, for there never was any music or any delight heard in Ireland to compare with that music of the swans. And they used to be telling stories, and to be talking with men of Ireland every day, and with their teachers and their fellow-pupils and their friends. And every night they used to sing very sweet music of the Sidhe; and every one that heard that music would sleep sound and quiet whatever trouble or long sickness might be on him; for every one that heard the music of the birds, it is happy and contented he would be after it.

FACTS & FANCY
DUBLIN

A thriving European metropolis, Dublin is the Republic of Ireland's largest city and its capital. Like Ireland, Dublin has wholeheartedly embraced the European Union over the past decade, benefiting greatly in doing so. With a young population and approximately half the country's citizens living within its boundaries, the streets are surprisingly crowded and nightlife is lively.

Founded by the Vikings in 841 as a fort from which they could better pillage monasteries, trade slaves and carry out general piracy, *Dubh Linn*, or "black pool," was named after the place where the Liffey and Poddle rivers came together.

Long after the Vikings surrendered to Brian Boru, and centuries after the Normans arrived, the British took over and oversaw a great blossoming of the city during what came to be known as the Georgian Period (approximately 1720–1820). Dublin, at that time, was the second city of the British Empire, only after London. Today, some of the best architecture of the era is evident in the row houses on Merrion Square, and the colorful Georgian doors scattered throughout the city have become famous landmarks.

Culture, naturally, plays a major role in the life of Dublin. After all, it has been pouring out of the city for centuries—from Jonathan Swift to Bono. Today, from the productions of the Abbey Theatre to the hopping Temple Bar area, there are always plenty of activities to take in.

Other sights not to be missed include the Book of Kells at Trinity College; the National Museum, housing many of the country's treasures; Grafton Street, for its shopping and people watching; the James Joyce Centre, and the GPO (the General Post Office where the famous Easter Uprising battle was fought in 1916). And while the countryside may beckon, don't forget to stay in the city long enough to stop at Guinness. Besides brewing the creamy stout, Guinness is also responsible for creating the world's most sold copyrighted book, *The Guinness Book of World Records.* ❧

Custom House, Dublin

The Rocky Road to Dublin

In the merry month of May from my home I started
Left the girls of Tuam nearly broken-hearted
Saluted Father dear, kissed my darlin' Mother
Drank a pint of beer my grief and tears to smother
Then off to reap the corn, and leave where I was born
I cut a stout blackthorn to banish ghost and goblin,
In a bran'new pair of brogues I rattled o'er the bogs
And frightened all the dogs on the rocky road to Dublin,

Chrorus
One, two, three, four five, hunt the hare and turn her
Down the rocky road, and all the ways to Dublin
Whack fol-lol-de-ra.

The Rocky Road to Dublin

In Mullingar that night I rested limbs so weary,
Started by daylight next morning light and airy,
Took a drop of the pure, to keep my heart from sinking,
That's an Irishman's cure, whene'er he's on for drinking,
To see the lasses smile, laughing all the while,
At my curious style, 'twould set your heart a-bubbling,
They ax'd if I was hired, the wages I required,
Till I was almost tired of the rocky road to Dublin.

   Chorus

In Dublin next arrived, I thought it such a pity,
To be so soon deprived a view of that fine city,
Then I took a stroll out among the quality,
My bundle it was stole in a neat locality;
Something crossed my mind, then I looked behind,
No bundle could I find upon me stick a-wobblin',
Enquiring for the rogue, they said my Connaught brogue
Wasn't much in vogue on the rocky road to Dublin.

   Chorus

176

The Rocky Road to Dublin

From there I got away my spirits never failing,
Landed on the quay as the ship was sailing,
Captain at me roared, said that no room had he,
When I jumped aboard, a cabin found for Paddy
Down among the pigs, I played some funny rigs
Danced some hearty jigs, the water round me bubblin'
When off to Holyhead I wished myself was dead,
Or better far, instead, on the rocky road to Dublin.

Chorus

The boys of Liverpool, when we safely landed,
Called myself a fool, I could no longer stand it;
Blood began to boil, temper I was losin'
Poor old Erin's isle they began abusin'
"Hurrah my soul!" sez I, my shillelagh I let fly,
Some Galway boys were by, saw I was a hobble in,
Then with a loud Hurrah, they joined in the affray,
We quickly cleared the way, for the rocky road to Dublin.

Chorus

177

"KILLY WHAT...
BALLY WHERE?"

Donegal, Kilkenny, Knockananna, Drogheda—how did they come up with these names?!? Over the millennia, Gaelic and Viking names have become anglicized; later, when the tables turned, English names became Gaelicized. This brief list will give some understanding of how a particular town got its name. Once again spelling isn't as important as pronunciation . . . which is almost impossible anyway.

ARD: a high place, either in importance or physically

BALLY: town; originally, an area belonging to a particular clan or tribe

BEG: small (often at the end of a name to distinguish it from a larger one nearby)

BUN: mouth of a river

CAHER or CASHEL: a fortified area

❋ CARRIK, CARRIG: a rock, or a castle built on a rock

❋ CLON, CLOON: dry place

❋ DERRY: place of oak trees or woods

❋ DROICHEAD: bridge

❋ DRUM, DROM: ridge

❋ DUN: fortified area, castle, or fortress

* GAL, GAEL: foreigner or stranger

* GLEN: a valley between mountains

* INNIS, INISH, ENNIS: island

* KILL or KIL: church or monastery

* KNOCK: hill

* KYLE: woods

* LIS: fort; sometimes associated with the fairies or little people

* LOUGH: lake

* MONEY, MONI: tree grove or bog

* MUCK, MUC, MUIC: pig or pigs

* OWEN: river

* RATH: fort or monastery

* ROS: wood

* SLIEVE: mountain

* TRA: beach

* TULLA, TULLY: little hill

O FOR A
BREATH
OF IRISH
AIR
AND A
SIGHT OF
THE IRISH
GREEN

A TASTE OF THE IRISH BILL OF FARE FROM THE HANDS OF MY IRISH COLEEN

CORNED BEEF AND PARSNIP

Corned beef and cabbage, it turns out, is an American invention (albeit an Irish American one), a substitution for a traditional dish called bacon and cabbage. Back in Ireland the dish is made with a bacon joint (not the cut of pork Americans think of as bacon), which was either unavailable in the United States or too expensive for the Irish immigrants. This is a traditional Irish dish that keeps the corned beef you may be used to, and adds a tasty potato and parsnip mash. It's perfect for St. Paddy's Day.

3 pounds corned beef brisket
2 celery stalks, chopped
1 carrot, chopped
2 leeks, chopped
1 teaspoon peppercorns
1¼ cups dry cider

1. Place the corned beef in a large pot. Add the chopped vegetables, peppercorns, and cider, and cover with cold water.
2. Bring to a boil over medium heat, and simmer for 2 hours (or 40 minutes per pound) until tender.

3. Remove the corned beef from the heat, allowing it to remain in its liquid until ready to serve. This will keep the meat warm while you make the sauce. You will need some of this liquid to make the sauce (see below), but you may discard the remainder of it as well as the vegetables when finished.
4. Slice the corned beef, serve the parsnip mash as a side dish, and put the sauce in a gravy dish—it's for the meat, but delicious with the mash, too.

Parsnip Mash

1 pound potatoes, peeled (or
   unpeeled if you like) and chopped
1 pound parsnips, peeled and chopped
$2/3$ cup mixture of milk and cream
2–3 tablespoons butter
2 tablespoons chopped scallions
Salt and pepper

1. Place the potatoes and parsnips in
   a large pot and cover with cold
   water. Boil until fork-tender.
2. Drain the potatoes/parsnips well,
   then mash with the milk, cream,
   and butter.
3. Mix in the scallions and add salt
   and pepper to taste.

Mustard and Cider Sauce

4 tablespoons butter
4 tablespoons flour
1 tablespoon mustard
$1^1/4$ cups cooking liquid (from
   corned beef)
Dash of cream

1. Melt the butter over medium heat
   and stir in the flour. Allow the
   mixture to cook for a few minutes, whisking constantly.
2. Add the mustard and whisk in the
   cooking liquid. Bring to a boil
   and simmer for 3 to 4 minutes.
3. Stir in the cream.

Yield: 4 servings.

May the
Fairies Luck
Go with You

The Legend of O'Donoghue

by T. Crofton Croker

I n an age so distant that the precise period is unknown, a chieftain named O'Donoghue ruled over the country which surrounds the romantic Lough Lean, now called the lake of Killarney. Wisdom, beneficence, and justice distinguished his reign, and the prosperity and happiness of his subjects were their natural results. He is said to have been as renowned for his warlike exploits as for his pacific virtues; and as a proof that his domestic administration was not the less rigorous because it was mild, a rocky island is pointed out to strangers, called "O'Donoghue's Prison," in which this prince once confined his own son for some act of disorder and disobedience.

His end—for it cannot correctly be called his death—was singular and mysterious. At one of those splendid feasts for which his court was celebrated, surrounded by the most distinguished of his

The Legend of O'Donoghue

subjects, he was engaged in a prophetic relation of the events which were to happen in ages yet to come. His auditors listened, now wrapt in wonder, now fired with indignation, burning with shame, or melted into sorrow, as he faithfully detailed the heroism, the injuries, the crimes, and the miseries of their descendants. In the midst of his predictions he rose slowly from his seat, advanced with a solemn, measured, and majestic tread to the shore of the lake, and walked forward composedly upon its unyielding surface. When he had nearly reached the center he paused for a moment, then, turning slowly round, looked toward his friends, and waving his arms to them with the cheerful air of one taking a short farewell, disappeared from their view.

The memory of the good O'Donoghue has been cherished by successive generations with affectionate reverence; and it is believed that at sunrise, on every Mayday morning, the anniversary of his departure, he revisits his ancient domains: a favored few only are in general permitted to see him, and this distinction is always an omen of good fortune to the beholders; when it is granted to many it is a sure token of an abundant harvest—a blessing, the want of which during this prince's reign was never felt by his people.

MYTHS & FOLK TALES

The Legend of O'Donoghue

Some years have elapsed since the last appearance of O'Donoghue. The April of that year had been remarkably wild and stormy; but on May-morning the fury of the elements had altogether subsided. The air was hushed and still; and the sky, which was reflected in the serene lake, resembled a beautiful but deceitful countenance, whose smiles, after the most tempestuous motions, tempted the stranger to believe that it belongs to a soul which no passion has ever ruffled.

The first beams of the rising sun were just gilding the lofty summit of Glenaa, when the waters near the eastern shore of the lake became suddenly and violently agitated, though all the rest of its surface lay smooth and still as a tomb of polished marble, the next morning a foaming wave darted forward, and, like a proud, high-crested war-horse, exulting in his strength, rushed across the lake toward

The Legend of O'Donoghue

Toomies mountain. Behind this wave appeared a stately warrior fully armed, mounted upon a milk-white steed that sprang after the wave along the water which bore him up like firm earth. The warrior was O'Donoghue, followed by numberless youths and maidens linked together by garlands of delicious spring flowers, and they timed their movements to strains of enchanting melody. When O'Donoghue had nearly reached the western side of the lake, he suddenly turned his steed, and directed his course along the wood-fringed shore of Glenaa, preceded by the huge wave that curled and foamed up as high as the horse's neck, whose fiery nostrils snorted above it. The long train of attendants followed with playful deviations the track of their leader, and moved on with unabated fleetness to their celestial music, till gradually, as they entered the narrow strait between Glenaa and Dinis, they became involved in the mists which still partially floated over the lakes, and faded from the view of the wondering beholders; but the sound of their music still fell upon the ear, and echo, catching up the harmonious strains, fondly repeated and prolonged them in soft and softer tones, till the last faint repetition died away, and the hearers awoke as from a dream of bliss.

Wearing of the Green

Oh! Paddy, dear, and did you hear the news that's goin'
'round,
The Shamrock is forbid by law, to grow on Irish ground;
Saint Patrick's day no more we'll keep, His color can't
be seen,
For there's a bloody law agin' the Wearin' o' the Green;
I met with Napper Tandy and he tuk me by the hand,
And he said "how's poor ould Ireland, and how does
she stand?"
She's the most distressful country, that ever you have seen;
They're hanging men and women there, for "Wearin' o' the
Green."

Then since the color we must wear, is England's cruel red,
Sure Ireland's sons will ne'er forget, the blood that they
have shed;

You may take the Shamrock from your hut, and cast it
    on the sod,
But 'twill take root and flourish still, 'tho' under foot
    'tis trod;
When the law can stop the blades of grass from growing
    as they grow,
And when the leaves in summer time, their verdure dare
    not show;
Then I will change the color I wear in my corbeen,
But 'till that day, please God, I'll stick to "Wearin' o' the Green."

But if at last our color should be torn from Ireland's heart,
Her sons with shame and sorrow from the dear old soil
    will part;
I've heard whisper of a country that lies far beyant the say,
Where rich, and poor, stand equal, in the light of freedom's day;
Oh, Erin must we lave you, driven by the tyrant's hand,
Must we ask a mother's welcome from a strange but happier
    land?
Where the cruel cross of England's thraldom never shall
    be seen,
And where, thank God, we'll live and die, still "Wearin' o'
    the Green."

BLOODY SUNDAY

On January 30, 1972, between 15,000 and 30,000 civilian Irish civil rights demonstrators (the number is disputed on both sides) marched in the Bogside area of Derry, Northern Ireland, toward the Guildhall, but were redirected to Free Derry Corner due to military barricades. The march, which was called to protest internment without trial (introduced by the British government in 1971), was "illegal" according to British government authorities. A small group of teenagers broke off from the main march and attacked the British barricade with stones and shouted insults at the troops, and a water cannon, tear gas, and rubber bullets were used to disperse the rioters. Such confrontations between soldiers and youths were common, but reports of an IRA sniper operating in the area were given to the British command center. One young man was shot and killed, and the violence escalated. Despite a cease-fire order from British officials, soldiers from the British army's 1st Parachute Regiment opened fire on the fleeing protesters, killing 13, 6 of whom were minors, and wounding a number of others. One man later died from wounds attributed to that shooting. Many witnesses, including bystanders and journalists, testified that those shot at were all unarmed, and five of those wounded were shot in the back. The British government held two separate inquiries into the events, the first of which found the soldiers not guilty of the 14 deaths and drew great criticism; the second has yet to report. ⁂

SINGER'S
SEWING MACHINES

Donegall Place, Belfast

GOING HOME

BY BRIAN MOORE

I am one of those wanderers. After the wartime years in North Africa and Italy, I worked in Poland for the United Nations, then emigrated to Canada, where I became a citizen before moving on to New York, and at last to California, where I have spent the greater part of my life.

And yet in all the years I have lived in North America I have never felt that it is my home. Annually, in pilgrimage, I go back to Paris and the French countryside and to London, the city which first welcomed me as a writer. And if I think of reemigrating it is to France or England, not to the place where I was born.

For I know that I cannot go back. Of course, over the years I have made many return visits to my native Belfast. But Belfast, its configuration changed by the great air raids of the blitz, its inner city covered with a carapace of flyovers, its new notoriety as a theater of violence, armed patrols and hovering helicopters, seems another city, a distant relative to that Belfast which in a graveyard in Connemara filled my mind with a jumbled kaleidoscope of images fond, frightening, surprising and sad.

—My pet canary is singing in its cage above my father's head as he sits reading *The Irish News* in the breakfast room of our house in Belfast—

—A shrill electric bell summons me to Latin class in the damp, hateful corri-

GOING HOME

dors of St. Malachy's College. I have forgotten the declension and hear the swish of a rattan cane as I hold out my hand for punishment—

—In Fortstewart, where we spent our summer holidays, I have been all day on the sands, building an elaborate sand sculpture in hopes of winning the Cadbury contest first prize, a box of chocolates—

—Alexandra Park, where, a seven-year-old, I walk beside my sister's pram holding the hand of my nurse, Nellie Ritchie, who at that time I secretly believed to be my real mother—

—I hear the terrified squeal of a pig dragged out into the yard for butchery on my uncle's farm in Donegal—

—I stand with my brothers and sisters singing a ludicrous Marian hymn in St. Patrick's Church at evening devotions:

> O Virgin pure, O spotless maid,
> We sinners send our prayers to thee,
> Remind thy Son that He has paid
> The price of our iniquity—

—I hear martial music, as a regimental band of the British Army marches out from the military barracks behind our house. I see the shining brass instruments, the drummers in tiger-skin aprons, the regimental mascot, a large horned goat.

GOING HOME

Behind that imperial panoply long lines of poor recruits are marched through the streets of our native city to board ship for India, a journey from which many will never return—

—Inattentive and bored, I kneel at the Mass amid the stench of unwashed bodies in our parish church, where 80 percent of the female parishioners have no money to buy overcoats or hats and instead wear black woolen shawls which cover head and shoulders, marking them as "Shawlies," the poorest of the poor—

—We, properly dressed in our middle-class school uniforms sitting in a crosstown bus, move through the poor streets of Shankill and the Falls, where children without shoes play on the cobbled pavements—

—The front gates of the Mater Infirmorum Hospital, where my father, a surgeon, is medical superintendent. As he drives out of those gates, a man so poor and desperate that he will court minor bodily injury to be given a bed and food for a few days steps in front of my father's car—

—An evening curfew is announced following Orange parades and the clashes which invariably follow them. The curfew, my father says, is less to prevent riots than to stop the looting of shops by both Catholic and Protestant poor—

—Older now, I sit in silent teen-age rebellion as I

GOING HOME

hear my elders talk complacently of the "Irish Free State" and the differences between the Fianna Fáil and Fine Gael parties who compete to govern it. Can't they see that this Catholic theocratic "grocer's republic" is narrow-minded, repressive and no real alternative to the miseries and injustices of Protestant Ulster? —

—Unbeknownst to my parents I stand on Royal Avenue hawking copies of a broadsheet called *The Socialist Appeal*, although I have refused to join the Trotskyite party which publishes it. Belfast and my childhood have made me suspicious of faiths, allegiances, certainties. It is time to leave home—

The kaleidoscope blurs. The images disappear. The past is buried until, in Connemara, the sight of Bulmer Hobson's grave brings back those faces, those scenes, those sounds and smells which now live only in my memory. And in that moment I know that when I die I would like to come home at last to be buried here in this quiet place among the grazing cows. ●

BRIAN MOORE (1921–1999) was born in Belfast, Northern Ireland, to a large Catholic family. Early in life, however, he rejected his faith and emigrated to Canada. He continued to travel throughout Europe, Canada, and the United States, and published 20 novels, many of which dealt with issues of cultural identity, loyalty, and conflicts surrounding Catholic life. "Going Home" is the last essay written before his death.

FACTS & FANCY
BELFAST

To many, the mere mention of Belfast—the capital of Northern Ireland and the island's second largest city—conjures up images of barbed wire and bombs. But since all sides came to agreement in 1998, Belfast is looking more like its prosperous Victorian self, leaving behind the "Troubles" that flared in the late 1960s. All that remains as a reminder of these terrible times are the political murals, which are among the most visited sites in the city. Those of the Protestants (who fought for a union with Great Britain) can be found in the Shankill Road neighborhood, while those of the Catholics (who want to join the rest of Ireland as one country) can be seen along Falls Road.

About 9,000 years before the troubles began, however, there was peace as the first people arrived in Belfast and settled around the River Farset (which gave the city its name, *Béal Feirste*, Irish for "mouth of the Farset"). Unfortunately, that river is no longer visible: It's been covered and now flows *under* the High Street, leaving the Lagan River alone to wind through the city above ground.

Over the millennia the Celts arrived, the Vikings came, St. Patrick passed through, and the English colonized. But Belfast really began to grow in the 17th century as it went through the Industrial Revolution. Over the next 300 years it prospered—even through the famine years that devastated the South—becoming rich on tobacco, rope making, linen, and shipbuilding. And while the shipbuilding industry was turning out vessels that included the infamous *Titanic*, the surrounding countryside supplied flax that yielded some of the most refined tablecloths in the world. That same countryside and the ruins of nearby Dunluce Castle also provided inspiration for Belfast native C. S. Lewis's *Narnia*.

Now, though the industries are greatly reduced (or gone altogether), the giant shipyard cranes—known locally as Sampson and Goliath—still dominate the skyline. The impressive Victorian buildings also remain, but today they are more likely to be chic hotels or fancy restaurants than factories turning out rope.

Belfast has once again become a vibrant, bustling city. One thing has remained as sharp as ever: the famous Irish wit. Asked about the locally built *Titanic*, a native was quoted as saying, "It was in fine shape when it left here." ❉

Castle Place, Belfast

The Boundary Commission
by Paul Muldoon

You remember that village where the border ran
Down the middle of the street,
With the butcher and baker in different states?
Today he remarked how a shower of rain

Had stopped so cleanly across Golightly's lane
It might have been a wall of glass
That had toppled over. He stood there, for ages,
To wonder which side, if any, he should be on.

May your hens get the disorder,
your cows the crippen, and
your calves the white scour, and
may you yourself go blind so
that you'll not know your
woman from a haystack.

May you find the bees but
miss the honey.

If ever you're on the pig's
back, I hope it's heading
for the curing house.

May your heifer never
get to the bull.

Curses!

IRISH CURSES!

May your spuds be like
rosary beads on the stalk.

May you never see the light
of heaven till you pay me
what you owe me.

May the devil behead all
landlords and make a day's
work of their necks.

May they all go to hell and
not have a drop of porter to
quench their eternal thirst.

May you break your kneecap
going down the steep steps of
your rosiest garden.

May you marry in haste and
repent at leisure.

A high noose and gallows and
a windy day outside to you.

Increasing calamity to you.

Six eggs to you and a
half dozen of them rotten.

When the last train leaves
for heaven may you still be
in the waiting room.

May the devil's dowser dip
his twig to your buttermilk.

May the only tears
at your graveside be
the onion pullers'.

That you may be left a hundred pounds and the will lost.

WORK is the curse of
the drinking class.

—Oscar Wilde

FACTS & FANCY
THE KING'S ENGLISH, MY ARSE!

High above the village of Blarney in the battlements of a 15th-century castle (that has seen better days) lies a magical stone. It is said that with one kiss of this stone you will receive the gift of eloquence. The question is, when you are using your new gift in the pubs of Blarney Village that night, will you understand what the punters are saying back to you?

Here is a short list of some common words and phrases you're likely to hear around Ireland (or around the Irish wherever they roam). So don't be a git, pull your socks up, and prepare for a good chinwag by studying the list. The locals will likely be gobsmacked at your talent, and it'll be grand.

AISY: slowly (easy)

ARSE: backside

BLAGGARD: someone who is full of it

BOLLOCKS: anyone you think is stupid

BOLLOXED: very drunk

BUCKETING: raining very heavily

CHEEK: disrespect

CHEESE ON YOUR CHIN: your fly is open

CHEESED OFF: angry

CHINWAG: a chat

CHIPPER: fish-and-chips shop

CHIPS: french fries

CLIPPINGS OF TIN: having little or no money, as in "He's living on clippings of tin"

CONKERS: chestnuts

COOKER: stove

CRAIC: (pronounced crack) fun time

CRISPS: potato chips

CULCHIE: a city dweller's name for a country person

DA: father

DOSSER: layabout, or useless person

Cormac Me Fieri Fecit an 1846

The King's English, My Arse!

EEJIT: idiot

FAG: cigarette

FAIR PLAY/WHACK TO YA: well done

FANNY: female genitalia

FECK: used instead of the other F word

FLUTHERED: drunk

FRY or FRY-UP: fried breakfast (sausage, bacon, eggs and black-and-white pudding)

GIT: rotten person

GOB: mouth, as in "Shut your gob"

GOBSHITE: idiot

GOBSMACKED: very surprised

GOING NINETY TO THE DOZEN: going very fast

GRAND: fine, lovely

HAVE A GO: take a turn, or engage in a fight

HER TONGUE WON'T LAST HER A LIFETIME: She has the gift of gab, and then some

HOLE IN THE WALL: ATM

HOOLEY: party, celebration

* HUNGER MAKES GOOD SAUCE: every-
* thing tastes good when you're hungry
* I COULD EAT A BABY'S ARSE
* THROUGH THE BARS OF A COT
* [crib]: I'm hungry
* I'D EAT A FARMER'S ARSE THROUGH
* A BLACKTHORN BUSH: I'm hungry
* IT'S TIME TO SPIT IN YOUR OWN
* ASHES: time to go home
* JACKEEN: a country person's name for
* somebody who lives in Dublin
* JACKS: toilet
* JAM ON YOUR EGG: wishful thinking/will
* never happen
* JAMMERS: very crowded, busy
* KIP: nap
* KNACKER: gypsy, traveling person
* KNACKERED: very tired
* LANGERED: falling-down drunk
* LASHING: raining hard
* THE LOCAL: the pub you frequent near
* your house

THE KING'S ENGLISH, MY ARSE!

LOCK IN: when a publican locks people in after hours so the pub looks closed from the outside

MESSAGES: shopping, groceries

MULCHIE or MUNCHIE: somebody who lives in the country

MUTTON DRESSED AS A LAMB: describes an older woman dressed inappropriately for her age; a bit of a slapper

NAPPY: diaper

PISS UP: to get drunk or boozing session, as in "They had a right good piss-up last night"

POGUE MAHONE: kiss my arse

POOF: homosexual

POTEEN: illegal spirits

PULL YOUR SOCKS UP: get to work/busy

QUEUE UP: form a line

RI-RA: fun and excitement

* ROSIE LEE: tea
* RUBBER: pencil eraser
* RUNNERS: trainers/sneakers/running shoes/tennis shoes
* SAMBOS: sandwiches
* SHAG: have sex
* SLAG: a promiscuous person
* SLÁINTE: cheers (literally "Health!")
* SLAPPER: person of low morals
* SNOG: to make out, kiss
* SNUG: pub booth
* THAT'S ARTHUR GUINNESS TALKING: the drink talking
* THREE SHEETS TO THE WIND: drunk
* TWISTIN' HAY: starting trouble, usually in a playful way
* TWO EGGS IN A HANKIE: colorful way to describe someone's arse
* WRECKED: tired
* YOUR MAN/WOMAN: that guy/woman
*

Blarney Castle

by Father Prout

There is a boat on the lake to float on,
And lots of beauties which I can't entwine;
But were I a preacher, or a classic teacher,
In every feature I'd make 'em shine!

There is a stone there, that whoever kisses,
O! he never misses to grow eloquent;
'Tis he may clamber to a lady's chamber,
Or become a member of parliament:

A clever spouter he'll soon turn out, or
An out-and-outer, "to be let alone."
Don't hope to hinder him, or to bewilder him,
Sure he's a pilgrim from the Blarney stone!

The Changeling

by Lady Francesca Speranza Wilde

A woman was one night lying awake while her husband slept, when the door suddenly opened and a tall dark man entered, of fierce aspect, followed by an old hag with a child in her arms—a little, misshapen, sickly-looking little thing. They both sat down by the fire to warm themselves, and after some time the man looked over at the cradle that stood beside the mother's bed with her boy in it, and kept his eyes on it for several minutes.

Then he rose, and when the mother saw him walking over direct to the cradle, she fainted and knew no more. When she came to herself she called to her husband, and bade him light a candle; thus he did, on which the old hag in the Corner rose up at once and blew it out. Then he lit it a second time, and it was blown out; and still a third time he lit the candle, when again it was blown out, and a great peal of laughter was heard in the darkness.

The Changeling

On this the man grew terribly angry, and taking up the tongs he made a blow at the hag; but she slipped away, and struck him on the arm with a stick she held in her hand. Then he grew more furious, and beat her on the head till she roared, when he pushed her outside and locked the door.

After this he lit the candle in peace; but when they looked at the cradle, lo! in place of their own beautiful boy, a hideous little creature, all covered with hair, lay grinning at them. Great was their grief and lamentation, and both the man and his wife wept and wailed aloud for the loss of their child, and the cry of their sorrow was bitter to hear.

Just then the door suddenly opened, and a young woman came in, with a scarlet handkerchief wound round her head.

"What are you crying for," she asked, "at this time of night, when every one should be asleep?"

"Look at this child in the cradle," answered the man, "and you will cease to wonder why we mourn and are sad at heart." And he told her all the story.

The Changeling

When the young woman went over to the cradle and looked at the child, she laughed, but said nothing.

"Your laughter is stranger than our tears," said the man. "Why do you laugh in the face of our sorrows?"

"Because," she said, "this is my child that was stolen from me to-night; for I am one of the fairy race, and my people, who live under the fort on the hill, thought your boy was a fine child, and so they changed the babies in the cradle; but after all I would rather have my own, ugly as he is, than any mortal child in the world. So now I'll tell you how to get back your own son, and I'll take away mine at once. Go to the old fort on the hill when the moon is full, and take with you three sheaves of corn and some fire, and burn them one after the other. And when the last sheaf is burning, an old man will come up through the smoke, and he will ask you what it is you desire. Then tell him you must have your child back, or you will burn down the fort, and leave no dwelling-place for his people on the hill. Now, the fairies cannot stand against the power of fire, and they will give you

The Changeling

back your child at the mere threat of burning the fort. But mind, take good care of him after, and tie a nail from a horse-shoe round his neck, and then he will be safe."

With that the young woman took up the ugly little imp from the cradle in her arms, and was away before they could see how she got out of the house.

Next night, when the moon was full, the man went to the old fort with the three sheaves of corn and the fire, and burned them one after the other; and as the second was lighted there came up an old man and asked him what was his desire.

"I must have my child again that was stolen," he answered, "or I'll burn down every tree on the hill, and not leave you a stone of the fort where you can shelter any more with your fairy kindred."

Then the old man vanished, and there was a great silence, but no one appeared.

On this the father grew angry, and he called out in a loud voice, "I am lifting the third sheaf now, and I'll burn

The Changeling

and destroy and make desolate your dwelling-place, if my child is not retuned."

Then a great tumult and clamour was heard in the fort, and a voice said, "Let it be. The power of the fire is too strong for us. Bring forth the child."

And presently the old man appeared, carrying the child in his arms.

"Take him," he said. "By the spell of the fire, and the corn you have conquered. But take my advice, draw a circle of fire, with a hot coal this night, round the cradle when you go home, and the fairy power cannot touch him any more, by reason of the fire."

So the man did as he was desired, and by the spell of fire and of corn the child was saved from evil, and he grew and prospered. And the old fort stands to this day safe from harm, for the man would allow no hand to move a stone or harm a tree; and the fairies still dance there on the rath, when the moon is full, to the music of the fairy pipes, and no one hinders them.

BUTTERMILK SCONES

Morning and afternoon tea (see page 22) in Ireland are often served with scones, brown bread (see page 71), soda bread (see page 96), delicious Irish butter, and jam.

2¹/₂ cups plain flour
¹/₂ cup whole wheat pastry flour
3 tablespoons sugar
¹/₂ teaspoon salt
1 teaspoon baking powder
1 teaspoon baking soda
1 teaspoon cream of tartar
¹/₄ cup unsalted butter, cut into
    small pieces
1 cup currants (or raisins)
1 teaspoon caraway seeds
1 cup buttermilk
1 egg, slightly beaten

1. Grease a baking sheet and pre-heat the oven to 375° F.
2. Blend the flours, sugar, salt, baking powder, baking soda, and cream of tartar.
3. Rub the butter into the dry ingredients until it is well distributed. Mix in the currants (or raisins) and caraway seeds.
4. In a separate bowl, whisk together the buttermilk and egg. Add this liquid mixture to the dry ingredients and mix until blended. Turn onto a floured board and knead for a minute or two.
5. Roll the dough flat to about ³/₄ inch thick. Cut it into circles and place them on the greased baking sheet, spacing about 3 inches apart.
6. Bake for 20 to 25 minutes or until golden brown. Cool slightly on a wire rack, and serve warm with a pot of jam and cup of tea.

Yield: 6–8 scones.

219

The Passing of the Gael
by Ethna Carbery

They are going, going, going from the valleys and the hills,
They are leaving far behind them heathery moor and mountain rills,
All the wealth of hawthorn hedges where the brown thrush sways
  and trills.

They are going, shy-eyed colleens and lads so straight and tall,
From the purple peaks of Kerry, from the crags of wild Imaal,
From the greening plains of Mayo and the glens of Donegal.

They are leaving pleasant places, shores with snowy sands outspread;
Blue and lonely lakes a-stirring when the wind stirs overhead;
Tender living hearts that love them, and the graves of kindred dead.

They shall carry to the distant land a tear-drop in the eye
And some shall go uncomforted—their days an endless sigh
For Kathaleen Ní Houlihan's sad face, until they die.

The Passing of The Gael

Oh, Kathaleen Ní Houlihan, your road's a thorny way,
And 'tis a faithful soul would walk the flints with you for aye,
Would walk the sharp and cruel flints until his locks grew gray.

So some must wander to the East, and some must wander West;
Some seek the white wastes of the North, and some Southern nest;
Yet never shall they sleep so sweet as on your mother breast.

The Passing of The Gael

The whip of hunger scourged them from the glens and quiet moors,
But there's a hunger of the heart that plenty never cures;
And they shall pine to walk again the rough road that is yours.

Within the city streets, hot, hurried, full of care,
A sudden dream shall bring them a whiff of Irish air—
A cool air, faintly-scented, blown soft from otherwhere.

Oh, the cabins long-deserted! Olden memories awake—
Oh, the pleasant, pleasant places!—Hush! the blackbird in the brake!
Oh, the dear and kindly voices!—Now their hearts are fain to ache.

They may win a golden store—sure the whins were golden too;
And no foreign skies hold beauty like the rainy skies they knew;
Nor any night-wind cool the brow as did the foggy dew.

They are going, going, going, and we cannot bid them stay;
The fields are now the strangers' where the strangers' cattle stray.
Oh! Kathaleen Ní Houlihan, your way's a thorny way!

A Bunch of Wild Thyme

Come all ye maidens young and fair
And you that are blooming in your prime
Always beware and keep your garden fair
Let no man steal away your thyme

    Chorus
    For thyme it is a precious thing
    And thyme brings all things to my mind
    Thyme with all its flavours, along with all its joys
    Thyme, brings all things to my mind

Once I and a bunch of thyme
I thought it never would decay
Then came a lusty sailor
Who chanced to pass my way
And stole my bunch of thyme away

    Chorus

The sailor gave to me a rose
A rose that never would decay
He gave it to me to keep me reminded
Of when he stole my thyme away

    Chorus

WHAT'S IN A NAME?

The Irish started using last names in the 11th century, becoming one of the first countries in the world to use the current hereditary system. Generally derived from Gaelic, Norman, Scottish, English, and even French, many last names began as a father's name or a trade name. *Mac* (or its abbreviation *Mc*) means "son of," while *O'* signifies "grandson of." Many of the *O*'s and *Macs* were dropped in the 17th century because, considering the political climate at the time, having a distinctly Irish name was, let's say, not an asset.

One category of name that is distinctly missing from Irish surnames (but is common in English ones) is the toponymic or place name. This is an indication that family ties and *who* you were descended from were far more important than *where* you came from.

Spelling can be tricky, especially if you are a New World Irishman whose possibly illiterate, thick-accented (maybe even non–English-speaking) relative passed through Ellis Island when the grumpy bureaucrat in charge of taking down his name was having a bad day. *O'Naghten* could become Norton, *O'Coigley* might be written as Quigley, so when doing research, remember to try several different spellings—with and without *O*'s, *Macs*, and *Mcs*.

COMMON IRISH NAMES AND THEIR MEANINGS

BRADY: spirited or large-chested

BRENNAN: sorrow

BROWN: son of the judge

BURKE: from Richard de Burgh

BYRNE: raven

CAMPBELL: crooked mouth

CLARKE: clergyman

COLLINS: young creature, puppy

CONNOLLY: valorous

DALY: present at assemblies

DOYLE: dark stranger

DUFFY: dark, black

DUNNE: brown

FITZGERALD: son of Gerald

FITZPATRICK: devotee of Saint Patrick

FLYNN: red or ruddy

FOLEY: plunderer

GALLAGHER: foreign help

HEALY: artistic, scientific, ingenious

HUGHES: fire

JOHNS(T)ON: son of John

KELLY: war, strife or bright-headed

KENNEDY: armored head or misshapen head

LYNCH: mariner

MACMAHON: strong or large man

MAGUIRE: pale colored

MARTIN/MACGILLMARTIN: devotee
    of Saint Martin

MCCARTHY: loving

MCGRATH: wealthy man

MOORE: dark skinned

MORAN: great

MURPHY: sea warrior

* MURRAY: seaman or by the sea

* NOLAN/KNOWLAN: noble or famous

* O'BRIEN: brave, virtuous

* O'CONNOR: dog or wolf lover

* O'DOHERTY: wicked

* O'NEILL: champion or cloud

* O'REILLY: a small stream

* O'SULLIVAN: little dark eye

* O'CALLAGHAN: bright headed

* O'CARROLL: valorous in battle

* O'CONNELL: strong as a wolf

* O'DONNELL: mighty

* O'FARRELL: brave man

* O'LEARY: calf keeper

* O'SHEA: stately, majestic

* POWER: poor man

* QUINN: chief

* RYAN: little king

* SMITH (MCGOWAN): Gowan is Scottish
*   for "smith"

* SWEENEY: pleasant

* THOM(P)SON: son of Thom

* WALSH: a person from Wales

* WHITE: of fair complexion

* WILSON (from MacLiam): son of William

GOING INTO EXILE

BY LIAM O'FLAHERTY

Towards dawn, when the floor was crowded with couples, arranged in fours, stamping on the floor and going to and fro, dancing the "Walls of Limerick," Feeney was going out to the gable when his son Michael followed him out. The two of them walked side by side about the yard over the grey sea pebbles that had been strewn there the previous day. They walked in silence and yawned without need, pretending to be taking the air. But each of them was very excited. Michael was taller than his father and not so thickly built, but the shabby blue serge suit that he had bought for going to America was too narrow for his broad shoulders and the coat was too wide around the waist. He moved clumsily in it and his hands appeared altogether too bony and big and red, and he didn't know what to do with them. During his twenty-one years of life he had never worn anything other than the homespun clothes of Inverara, and the shop-made clothes appeared as strange to him and as uncomfortable as a dress suit worn by a man working in a sewer. His face was flushed a bright red and his blue eyes shone with excitement. Now and again he wiped the perspiration from his forehead with the lining of his grey tweed cap.

At last Patrick Feeney reached his usual position at the gable end. He halted, balanced himself on his heels with his hands in his waist belt, coughed and said,

228

"It's going to be a warm day." The son came up beside him, folded his arms and leaned his right shoulder against the gable.

"It was kind of Uncle Ned to lend the money for the dance, father," he said. "I'd hate to think that we'd have to go without something or other, just the same as everybody else has. I'll send you that money the very first money I earn, father . . . even before I pay Aunt Mary for my passage money. I should have all that money paid off in four months, and then I'll have some more money to send you by Christmas."

And Michael felt very strong and manly recounting what he was going to do when he got to Boston, Massachusetts. He told himself that with his great strength he would earn a great deal of money. Conscious of his youth and his strength and lusting for adventurous life, for the moment he forgot the ache in his heart that the thought of leaving his father inspired in him.

The father was silent for some time. He was look-ing at the sky with his lower lip hanging, thinking of nothing. At last he sighed as a memory struck him. "What is it?" said the son. "Don't weaken, for God's sake. You will only make it hard for me." "Fooh!" said the father suddenly with pretended gruffness. "Who is weakening? I'm afraid that your new clothes make

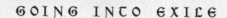

you impudent." Then he was silent for a moment and continued in a low voice: "I was thinking of that potato field you sowed alone last spring the time I had the influenza. I never set eyes on that man that could do it better. It's a cruel world that takes you away from the land that God made you for."

"Oh, what are you talking about, father?" said Michael irritably. "Sure what did anybody ever get out of the land but poverty and hard work and potatoes and salt?"

"Ah, yes," said the father with a sigh, "but it's your own, the land, and over there"—he waved his hand at the western sky—"you'll be giving your sweat to some other man's land, or what's equal to it."

"Indeed," muttered Michael, looking at the ground with a melancholy expression in his eyes, "it's poor encouragement you are giving me."

They stood in silence fully five minutes. Each hungered to embrace the other, to cry, to beat the air, to scream with excess sorrow. But they stood silent and somber, like nature about them, hugging their woe. ●

LIAM O'FLAHERTY (1896–1984) was born on the Aran Islands, which provided material for most of his writing. He lived the life of a fictional character—he studied for the priesthood, served in World War I, joined the Republicans during the Civil War, cut lumber in Canada, taught in Rio de Janeiro, and spoke out for the Irish Communist Party. He wrote more than a dozen novels and several collections of short stories.

After a Childhood
away from Ireland
by Eavan Boland

One summer
we slipped in at dawn
on plum-coloured water
in the sloppy quiet.
The engines
of the ship stopped.
There was an eerie
drawing near,
a noiseless, coming head-on
of red roofs, walls,
dogs, barley stooks.
Then we were there.
Cobh.

Coming home.
I had heard of this:
the ground the emigrants
resistless, weeping
laid their cheeks to,

put their lips to kiss.
Love is also memory.
I only stared.
What I had lost
was not land,
but the habit
of land,
whether of growing out of

Or settling back on
or being defined by.
I climb
to your nursery.
I stand listening
to the dissonances

Of the summer's day ending.
I bend to kiss you.
Your cheeks are brick pink.
They store warmth like clay.

FACTS & FANCY
MAEWYN SUCCAT

A lthough the name Maewyn Succat may not ring a bell (or bring to mind anything the least bit Irish), it should, because it is the given name of one of the most celebrated of all Irishmen: Saint Patrick.

Born somewhere on the west coast of Britain around the year a.d. 390 to Roman Christian aristocrats, Maewyn's life took a dramatic and fateful turn when he was captured by Irish marauders at age 16. Taken to Ireland and sold as a slave to a Druid high priest, young Maewyn was put to work in the cold and lonely fields as a shepherd. There, according to his book *Confessio*, he "was roused to prayer . . . whether there was snow or ice or rain . . . the spirit was then fervent within me."

Six years after being enslaved, Maewyn escaped his captors, taking with him not only his newfound faith in Christianity, but also a complete familiarity with Druid beliefs and lifestyle and fluency in the Irish language—knowledge that would serve his future mission perfectly.

Maewyn went to Auxerre, France, where he spent years studying under Saint Germanus. Pope Celestine I, renaming him Patrick, charged him with the task of converting pagan Ireland to Christianity. Patrick's writings tell us that he traveled the entire country, making converts and establishing churches and schools, and that he was seized at least a dozen times, once even being sentenced to death.

Although legend has it that Patrick drove the snakes out of Ireland, there were, in fact, never any snakes on the island, since it separated from mainland Britain before snakes could get there.

Nonetheless, Patrick remains the patron saint of the fear of snakes, excluded people, Ireland, New York, and Poona, India. ✾

CRUBEENS (PIG'S TROTTERS)

*T*his dish first gained popularity with factory workers in the 19th century, but was still found boiling away in big pots at markets around Ireland up until the 1940s. Nowadays this working-class meal has largely been replaced by McDonald's or batter burgers & chips, leaving pig's feet to be found only in the most traditional of butcher shops. No utensils are needed when eating crubeens.

6 pig's feet
1 onion stuck with 6 cloves
2 carrots
1 stalk celery
1 bay leaf
12 peppercorns
Salt
1 bunch parsley
1 sprig thyme

1. Place all the ingredients into a heavy pot or Dutch oven and pour in enough water to barely cover them.
2. Gently bring to a boil, then reduce the heat and simmer for at least 3 hours, until the meat is soft and very tender.

Yield: 2 servings.

Serve hot with mustard, soda bread (see page 96), and a hearty stout, or serve cold the next day for lunch.

The Silkie Wife

by Patrick Kennedy

hose in Shetland and Orkney Islands who know no better, are persuaded that the seals, or silkies, as they call them, can doff their coverings at times, and disport themselves as men and women. A fisher once turning a ridge of rock, discovered a beautiful bit of green turf adjoining the shingle, sheltered by rocks on the landward side, and over this turf and shingle two beautiful women chasing each other. Just at the man's feet lay two seal-skins, one of which he took up to examine it. The women, catching sight of him, screamed out, and ran to get possession of the skins. One seized the article on the ground, donned it in a thrice, and plunged into the sea; the other wrung her hands, cried, and begged the fisher to restore her property; but he wanted a wife, and would not throw away the chance. He wooed her so earnestly and lovingly, that she put on some woman's clothing which he brought her from his cottage, followed him home, and became his wife. Some years later, when their home was enlivened by the presence of two children, the husband awaking one night, heard voices in conversation from the kitchen.

The Silkie Wife

Stealing softly to the room door, he heard his wife talking in a low tone with some one outside the window. The interview was just at an end, and he had only time to ensconce himself in bed, when his wife was stealing across the room. He was greatly disturbed, but determined to do or say nothing till he should acquire further knowledge. Next evening, as he was returning home by the strand, he spied a male and female phoca sprawling on a rock a few yards out at sea. The rougher animal, raising himself on his tail and fins, thus addressed the astonished man in the dialect spoken in these islands:—"You deprived me of her whom I was to make my companion; and it was only yesternight that I discovered her outer garment, the loss of which obliged her to be your wife. I bear no malice, as you were kind to her in your own fashion; besides, my heart is too full of joy to hold any malice. Look on your wife for the last time." The other seal glanced at him with all the shyness and sorrow she could force into her now uncouth features; but when the bereaved husband rushed toward the rock to secure his lost treasure, she and her companion were in the water on the other side of it in a moment, and the poor fisherman was obliged to return sadly to his motherless children and desolate home.

ON STELLA's Birthday, 1719

by Jonathan Swift

Stella this day is thirty-four,
(We shan't dispute a year or more)
However Stella, be not troubled,
Although thy size and years are doubled,

Since first I saw thee at sixteen
The brightest virgin on the green,
So little is thy form declined
Made up so largely in thy mind.
Oh, would it please the gods to split
Thy beauty, size, and years, and wit,
No age could furnish out a pair
Of nymphs so graceful, wise and fair
With half your wit, your years and size:
And then before it grew too late,
How should I beg of gentle Fate,
(That either nymph might have her swain,)
To split my worship too in twain.

HOMESICKNESS

BY GEORGE MOORE

As well as the great lake there was a smaller lake in the bog where the villagers cut their turf. This lake was famous for its pike, and the landlord allowed Bryden to fish there, and one evening when he was looking for a frog with which to bait his line he met Margaret Dirken driving home the cows for the milking. Margaret was the herdsman's daughter, and lived in a cottage near the Big House; but she came up to the village whenever there was a dance, and Bryden had found himself opposite to her in the reels. But until this evening he had had little opportunity of speaking to her, and he was glad to speak to someone, for the evening was lonely, and they stood talking together.

"You're getting your health again," she said, "and will be leaving us soon."

"I'm in no hurry."

"You're grand people over there; I hear a man is paid four dollars a day for his work."

"And how much," said James, "has he to pay for his food and for his clothes?"

Her cheeks were bright and her teeth were small, white, and beautifully even; and a woman's soul looked at Bryden out of her soft Irish eyes. He was troubled and turned aside, and catching sight of a frog looking at him out of a tuft of grass, he said:

HOMESICKNESS

"I have been looking for a frog to put upon my pike line."

The frog jumped right and left, and nearly escaped in some bushes, but he caught it and returned with it in his hand.

"It is just the kind of frog a pike will like," he said. "Look at its great white belly and its bright yellow back."

And without more ado he pushed the wire to which the hook was fastened through the frog's fresh body, and dragging it through the mouth he passed the hooks through the hind legs and tied the line to the end of the wire.

"I think," said Margaret, "I must be looking after my cows; it's time I got them home."

"Won't you come down to the lake while I set my line?"

She thought for a moment and said:

"No, I'll see you from here."

He went down to the reedy tarn, and at his approach several snipe got up, and they flew above his head uttering sharp cries. His fishing rod was a long hazel stick, and he threw the frog as far as he could in the lake. In doing this he roused some wild ducks; a mallard and two ducks got up, and they flew towards the larger lake in a line with an old castle; and they had not disappeared from view when Bryden came towards her, and he and she drove the cows home together that evening.

They had not met very often when she said: "James, you had better not come here so often calling to me."

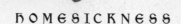

HOMESICKNESS

"Don't you wish me to come?"

"Yes, I wish you to come well enough, but keeping company isn't the custom of the country, and I don't want to be talked about."

"Are you afraid the priest would speak against us from the altar?"

"He has spoken against keeping company, but it is not so much what the priest says, for there is no harm in talking."

"But if you're going to be married there is no harm in walking out together."

"Well, not so much, but marriages are made differently in these parts; there isn't much courting here."

And next day it was known in the village that James was going to marry Margaret Dirken.

Never in the village of Duncannon had a young couple begun life with so much prospect of success, and some time after Christmas was spoken of as the best time for the marriage; James Bryden said that he would not be able to get his money out of America before the spring. The delay seemed to vex him, and he seemed anxious to be married, until one day he received a letter from America, from a man who had served in the bar with him. This friend wrote to ask Bryden if he were coming back. The letter was no more than a passing wish to see Bryden again. Yet Bryden stood looking at it, and everyone wondered what could be in the letter. It seemed momentous, and they hardly believed him when he said it was from a friend who wanted to know if his health were better. He tried to forget the

letter, and he looked at the
worn fields, divided by walls of loose
stones, and a great longing came upon him.

The smell of the Bowery slum had come
across the Atlantic, and had found him out in his
western headland; and one night he awoke from a dream in
which he was hurling some drunken customer through the
open doors into the darkness. He had seen his friend in his
white duck jacket throwing drink from glass into glass
amid the din of voices and strange
accents; he had heard the clang of
money as it was swept into the till, and
his sense sickened for the barroom. But
how should he tell Margaret Dirken that
he could not marry her? She had
built her life upon this marriage. He could not tell
her that he would not
marry her . . . yet he
must go. He felt as if he
were being hunted; the

HOMESICKNESS

thought that he must tell Margaret that he could not marry her hunted him day after day as a weasel hunts a rabbit. Again and again he went to meet her with the intention of telling her that he did not love her, that their lives were not for one another, that it had all been a mistake, and that happily he had found out it was a mistake soon enough. But Margaret, as if she guessed what he was about to speak of, threw her arms about him and begged him to say he loved her, and that they would be married at once. He agreed that he loved her, and that they would be married at once. But he had not left her many minutes before the feeling came upon him that he could not marry her—that he must go away. The smell of the barroom hunted him down. Was it for the sake of the money that he might make there that he wished to go back? No, it was not the money. What then? His eyes fell on the bleak country, on the little fields divided by bleak walls; he remembered the pathetic ignorance of the people, and it was these things that he could not endure. It was the priest who came to forbid the dancing. Yes, it was the priest. As he stood looking at the line of the hills the barroom seemed by him. He heard the politicians, and the excitement of politics was in his blood again. He must go away from this place—he must get back to the barroom. Looking up, he saw the scanty orchard, and he hated the spare road that led to the village, and he hated the little hill at the top of which the village began, and he hated more than all other places the house where he was to live with Margaret Dirken—if he married her. He could see it

ḤOMESICKNESS

from where he stood by the edge of the lake, with twenty acres of pasture land about it, for the landlord had given up part of his demesne land to them.

He caught sight of Margaret, and he called her to come through the stile.

"I have just had a letter from America."

"About the money?"

"Yes, about the money. But I shall have to go over there."

He stood looking at her, wondering what to say; and she guessed that he would tell her that he must go to see America before they were married.

"Do you mean, James, you will have to go at once?"

"Yes," he said, "at once. But I shall come back in time to be married in August. It will only mean delaying our marriage a month."

They walked on a little way talking, and every step he took James felt that he was step nearer the Bowery slum. And when they came to the gate Bryden said:

"I must walk on or I shall miss the train."

"But," she said, "you are not going now—you are not going today?"

"Yes, this morning. It is seven miles. I shall have to hurry not to miss the train."

And then she asked him if he would ever come back.

"Yes," he said, "I am coming back."

"If you are coming back, James, why don't you let me go with you?"

247

ḦOMESICKNESS

"You couldn't walk fast enough. We should miss the train."

"One moment, James. Don't make me suffer; tell me the truth. You are not coming back. Your clothes—where shall I send them?"

He hurried away, hoping he would come back. He tried to think that he liked the country he was leaving, that it would be better to have a farmhouse and live there with Margaret Dirken than to serve drinks behind a counter in the Bowery. He did not think he was telling her a lie when he said he was coming back. Her offer to forward his clothes touched his heart, and at the end of the road he stood and asked himself if he should go back to her. He would miss the train if he waited another minute, and he ran on. And he would have missed the train if he had not met a car. Once he was on the car he felt himself safe—the country was already behind him. The train and the boat at Cork were mere formulae; he was already in America.

And when the tall skyscraper stuck up beyond the harbor he felt the thrill of home that he had not found in his native village and wondered how it was that the smell of the bar seemed more natural that the smell of fields, and the roar of crowds more welcome than the silence of the lake's edge. He entered into negotiations for the purchase of the barroom. He took a wife, she bore him sons and daughters, the barroom prospered, property came and went; he grew old, his wife died, he retired from business, and reached the age when a man begins to feel there are not many years in front of him, and that all he has

248

HOMESICKNESS

had to do in life has been done. His children married, lonesomeness began to creep about him in the evening, and when he looked into the firelight, a vague tender reverie floated up, and Margaret's soft eyes and name vivified the dusk. His wife and children passed out of mind, and it seemed to him that a memory was the only real thing he possessed, and the desire to see Margaret again grew intense. But she was an old woman, she had married, maybe she was dead. Well, he would like to be buried in the village where he was born.

There is an unchanging, silent life within every man that none knows but himself, and his unchanging silent life was his memory of Margaret Dirken. The barroom was forgotten and all that concerned it, and the things he saw most clearly were the green hillside, and the bog lake and the rushes about it, and the greater lake in the distance, and behind it the blue line of wandering hills. ●

GEORGE MOORE (1852–1933) was born in Ireland and reared in affluence and boarding schools in County Mayo. At the age of 21, he moved to Paris to study painting but quickly abandoned the prospect for the love of literature. In 1880 he moved to London and wrote several novels there. Moore returned to Ireland in 1898 and helped found the Irish Literary Theater with William Butler Yeats, Edward Martyn, and Lady Gregory.

An Irish Love Song

By John Todhunter

O, you plant the pain in my heart with your wistful eyes,
    Girl of my choice, Maureen!
Will you drive me mad for the kisses your shy sweet mouth denies,
    Maureen!

Like a walking ghost I am, and no words to woo,
    White rose of the West, Maureen;
For it's pale you are, and the fear that's on you is over me too
    Maureen!

Sure it's our complaint that's on us, asthore, this day,
    Bride of my dreams, Maureen;
The smart of the bee that stung us, his honey must cure, they say,
    Maureen!

I'll coax the light to your eyes, and the rose to your face,
　　Mavourneen, my own Maureen,
When I feel the warmth of your breast, and your nest
　　　　is my arm's embrace,
　　Maureen!

O where was the King o' the
　　　　World that day—only me,
My one true love, Maureen,
And you the Queen with me
　　　　there, and your throne
　　　　in my heart,
　　　　machree,
　　Maureen!

FACTS & FANCY
"FILLIMS"

TURNING GREEN (2005, USA/Ireland) Comedy. Timothy Hutton in an indie film revolving around an orphaned American sent to live with his aunts in 1970s Ireland.

BREAKFAST ON PLUTO (2005, Ireland) Comedy/drama. Famed Irish director Neil Jordan's story of a transvestite cabaret performer who is the son of the local priest.

THE BOYS AND GIRL FROM COUNTY CLARE (2005, Ireland) Comedy. A bittersweet tale of sibling rivalry and musical competition set in Ireland.

BLOODY SUNDAY (2002, UK/Ireland) Documentary-style drama about one of the bloodiest days of the Irish "Troubles."

IN AMERICA (2002, Ireland) Drama/ romance. An Irish family arrives in New York City in the early 1980s in pursuit of the American dream and find plenty of adventure instead.

THIS IS MY FATHER (1999, Ireland/ Canada) Drama/romance. James Caan travels to Ireland in search of his real father.

ANGELA'S ASHES (1999, USA/Ireland) Drama. Grim story of an impoverished childhood in a time of desperation.

WAKING NED DEVINE (1998, Ireland) Comedy. Ned dies of shock when he wins the lottery, so his friends try to collect the winnings.

DANCING AT LUGHNASA (1997, Ireland/ UK/USA) Drama. Five unmarried sisters and their lives in 1930s Ireland, starring Meryl Streep.

THE MATCHMAKER (1997, Ireland/UK/ USA) Comedy. Janeane Garofalo finds herself

"FILLIMS"

in Ireland in the middle of a matchmaking festival.

MICHAEL COLLINS (1996, USA/Ireland) Drama. Julia Roberts, Liam Neeson, Aidan Quinn fight for Ireland's independence.

THE VAN (1996, UK/Ireland) Comedy. The third part of Roddy Doyle's Barrytown trilogy. (*The Commitments* and *The Snapper* are parts 1 and 2)

CIRCLE OF FRIENDS (1995, Ireland/USA/UK) Drama. Minnie Driver is one of three girlhood friends coming of age in 1950s Ireland.

THE BROTHERS MCMULLEN (1995, USA) Drama. Irish-Catholic brothers on Long Island have relationship problems.

THE SECRET OF ROAN INISH (1994, USA/Ireland) Fable. A fairy tale of Ireland's myths and historical struggles.

IN THE NAME OF THE FATHER (1993, Ireland/UK) Drama/biopic about Gerry Conlon, nominated for seven Oscars.

"FILLIMS"

THE SNAPPER (1993, Ireland) Comedy. The second of Roddy Doyle's hilarious Barrytown trilogy. (*The Commitments* and *The Van* are the other two).

THE CRYING GAME (1992, UK/Ireland) Drama. Neil Jordan's thriller about the relationship between an IRA terrorist and his captive British soldier.

THE COMMITMENTS (1991, Ireland) Comedy. Roddy Doyle's first in the Barrytown trilogy (beside *The Snapper* and *The Van*) combines great music with touching laughs.

MILLER'S CROSSING (1990, USA) Crime drama/thriller. The Coen brothers' take on Irish-American mobsters during prohibition.

MY LEFT FOOT (1989, Ireland/UK) Biopic/drama. Story of a spastic quadriplegic who uses his left foot to write.

DA (1988, USA) Drama. A New York playwright travels to Ireland to bury his "Da."

THE DEAD (1987, UK/USA/Ireland) Drama. Anjelica Huston stars in her father, director John Huston's last film; based on the James Joyce short story billed as a vast, merry, and uncommon tale of love.

RYAN'S DAUGHTER (1970, UK) Drama. Intrigue set in the Dingle peninsula in 1916, starring Robert Mitchum and Trevor Howard.

FINIAN'S RAINBOW (1968, USA) Musical. Francis Ford Coppola directs Fred Astair and Petula Clark (as an Irish father and daughter) who arrive in the rural South, followed by a leprechaun. How are things in Glocca Morra?

DARBY O'GILL AND THE LITTLE PEOPLE (1959, USA) Disney. When Darby finally catches the leprechaun, he's granted three wishes, all of which backfire.

SHAKE HANDS WITH THE DEVIL (1959, Ireland/USA) Drama. James Cagney, Glynnis Johns star in this battle between the IRA and the Brits.

"FILLIMS"

THE RISING OF THE MOON (1957, Ireland/USA) Comedy/drama. John Ford directs three stories of rural Irish life.

UNTAMED (1955, USA) Adventure. Tyrone Power, Susan Hayward leave the Emerald Isle for South Africa as the famine hits.

THE QUIET MAN (1952, USA) Drama/romance/comedy. Ex-boxer John Wayne returns to Ireland and meets his match, Maureen O'Hara, in this double Academy-award winner.

THE LUCK OF THE IRISH (1948, USA) Fantasy/comedy. A reporter meets a leprechaun and a girl while traveling in Ireland.

MY WILD IRISH ROSE (1947, USA) Musical. The story of Irish tenor Chauncey Olcott's life from childhood to stardom.

ODD MAN OUT (1947, UK) Drama/film noir. James Mason, leader of an Irish rebel organization, plans a holdup that goes wrong.

* I SEE A DARK STRANGER (1946, UK)
* Drama/thriller. Deborah Kerr gets mixed up
* with the IRA, Nazis, and a British officer
* played by Trevor Howard.
*
* THE BELLS OF ST. MARY'S (1945, USA)
* Drama. Bing Crosby reprises his role as
* Father Chuck O'Malley (from 1944's *Going*
* *My Way*), this time he is pitted against Ingrid
* Bergman as Sister Mary Benedict. The tag
* line, "Your heart will be wearing a smile!"
* says it all.
*
* GOING MY WAY (1944, USA) Musical.
* Singing Irish-Catholic priest Bing Crosby
* saves the church from all kinds of problems.
*
* LITTLE NELLIE KELLY (1940, USA) Musical.
* Judy Garland plays the Irish Nellie, who dies
* in childbirth, leaving her father and husband
* to raise her daughter.
*
* THE INFORMER (1935, USA) Drama.
* Two-time Oscar winner about the 1922
* Sinn Fein uprising.

AUNT EILEEN'S MINCE PIE

Although this is my grandmother's recipe, Aunt Eileen is the one famous in our family for bringing the underappreciated mince pie to Christmas. "Ewww!" we kids would say, "how can you eat that"—as if the chemical-laden nondairy whipped topping we'd been scarfing down was gourmet eats. Let's just say my tastes have matured. This past year, in fact, it was me who brought the mince pie to my sister's Christmas dinner. Naturally, being Irish-born, my niece Alannah and nephew Finn loved it!

1 pound round steak, chopped
4 Granny Smith apples, peeled, cored, and cubed
1/3 cup granulated sugar (to taste)
1/2 teaspoon ground cloves
1/2 teaspoon ground cinnamon
1/2 teaspoon ground nutmeg
1/2 teaspoon ground allspice
1/4 teaspoon salt
1/2 cup orange juice (or to taste)
1/2 cup raisins
1/2 cup currants
1/2 cup sweet pickle juice (to taste)
4 ounces candied citron
4 ounces candied lemon peel
1/4 cup brandy (or to taste)
1 9-inch double-crust pie pastry

1. Preheat the oven to 350° F.
2. Cook the chopped steak over medium heat in a skillet until browned. Set aside on a paper towel to drain.
3. Place all the filling ingredients in a medium-size pot (3 to 4 quarts), and add the drained meat.
4. Cook over medium heat, stirring occasionally, until the apples are tender.
5. Place the filling in the prepared pie shell. Cover with the top crust and make a small steam hole in the middle. Bake for about 1 hour or until the crust is slightly brown.

Yield: 1 pie.

259

The Little Waves of Breffny

by Eva Gore-Booth

The grand road from the mountain goes shining to the sea,
And there is traffic in it and many a horse and cart,
But the little roads of Cloonagh are dearer far to me,
And the little roads of Cloonagh go rambling through my heart.

A great storm from the ocean goes shouting o'er the hill,
And there is glory in it and terror on the wind,
But the haunted air of twilight is very strange and still,
And the little winds of twilight are dearer to my mind.

The great waves of the Atlantic sweep storming on their way,
Shining green and sliver with the hidden herring shoal,
But the Little Waves of Breffny have drenched my heart in spray,
And the Little Waves of Breffny go stumbling through my soul.

RIDERS TO THE SEA

By J. M. Synge

MAURYA (*an old woman*)
BARTLEY (*her son*)
CATHLEEN (*her daughter*)
NORA (*a younger daughter*)
MEN and **WOMEN**

SCENE. *An Island off the West of Ireland. (Cottage kitchen, with nets, oil-skins, spinning wheel, some new boards standing by the wall, etc.* **CATHLEEN**, *a girl of about twenty, finishes kneading cake, and puts it down in the pot-oven by the fire; then wipes her hands, and begins to spin at the wheel.* **NORA**, *a young girl, puts her head in at the door.*)

NORA (*in a low voice*) Where is she?

CATHLEEN She's lying down, God help her, and may be sleeping, if she's able.

[**NORA** *comes in softly, and takes a bundle from under her shawl.*]

CATHLEEN (*spinning the wheel rapidly*) What is it you have?

NORA The young priest is after bringing them. It's a shirt and a plain stocking were got off a drowned man in Donegal.

[**CATHLEEN** *stops her wheel with a sudden movement, and leans out to listen.*]

NORA We're to find out if it's Michael's they are, some time herself will be down looking by the sea.

CATHLEEN How would they be

Michael's, Nora. How would he go the length of that way to the far north?

NORA The young priest says he's known the like of it. "If it's Michael's they are," says he, "you can tell herself he's got a clean burial by the grace of God, and if they're not his, let no one say a word about them, for she'll be getting her death," says he, "with crying and lamenting."

[The door which **NORA** *half closed is blown open by a gust of wind.]*

CATHLEEN *(looking out anxiously)* Did you ask him would he stop Bartley going this day with the horses to the Galway fair?

NORA "I won't stop him," says he, "but let you not be afraid. Herself does be saying prayers half through the night, and the Almighty God won't leave her destitute," says he, "with no son living."

CATHLEEN Is the sea bad by the white rocks, Nora?

NORA Middling bad, God help us. There's a great roaring in the west, and it's worse it'll be getting when the tide's turned to the wind. *(She goes over to the table with the bundle.)* Shall I open it now?

CATHLEEN Maybe she'd wake up on us, and come in before we'd done. *(Coming to the table.)* It's a long time we'll be, and the two of us crying.

NORA *(goes to the inner door and listens)* She's moving about on the bed. She'll be coming in a minute.

CATHLEEN Give me the ladder, and I'll put them up in the turf-loft, the way she won't know of them at all, and maybe when the tide turns she'll be going down to see would he be floating from the east.

[They put the ladder against the gable of the chimney; CATHLEEN *goes up a few steps and hides the bundle in the turf-loft.* MAURYA *comes from the inner room.]*

MAURYA (*looking up at* CATHLEEN *and speaking querulously*) Isn't it turf enough you have for this day and evening?

CATHLEEN There's a cake baking at the fire for a short space (*throwing down the turf*) and Bartley will want it when the tide turns if he goes to Connemara.

*[*NORA *picks up the turf and puts it round the pot-oven]*

MAURYA (*sitting down on a stool at the fire*) He won't go this day with the wind rising from the south and west. He won't this day, for the young priest will stop him surely.

NORA He'll not stop him, mother, and I heard Eamon Simon and Stephen Pheety and Colum Shawn saying he would go.

MAURYA Where is he itself?

NORA He went down to see would there be another boat sailing in the week, and I'm thinking it won't be long till he's here now, for the tide's turning at the green head, and the hooker's tacking from the east.

CATHLEEN I hear some one passing the big stones.

NORA (*looking out*) He's coming now, and he in a hurry.

BARTLEY (*comes in and looks round the room. Speaking sadly and quietly*) Where is the bit of new rope, Cathleen, was bought in Connemara?

CATHLEEN (*coming down*) Give it to

him, Nora; it's on a nail by the white boards. I hung it up this morning, for the pig with the black feet was eating it.

NORA (*giving him a rope*) Is that it, Bartley?

MAURYA You'd do right to leave that rope, Bartley, hanging by the boards. (**BARTLEY** *takes the rope*) It will be wanting in this place, I'm telling you, if Michael is washed up tomorrow morning, or the next morning, or any morning in the week, for it's a deep grave we'll make him by the grace of God.

BARTLEY (*beginning to work with the rope*) I've not halter the way I can ride down on the mare, and I must go now quickly. This is the one boat going for two weeks or beyond it, and the fair will be a good fair for horses I heard them saying below.

MAURYA It's a hard thing they'll be saying below if the body is washed up and there's no man in it to make the coffin, and I after giving a big price for the finest white boards you'd find in Connemara.

[*She looks round at the boards.*]

BARTLEY How would it be washed up, and we after looking each day for nine days, and a strong wind blowing a while back from the west and south?

MAURYA If it wasn't found itself, that wind is raising the sea, and there was a star up against the moon, and it rising in the night. If it was a hundred horses, or a thousand horses you had itself, what is the price of a thousand horses against a son where there is one son only?

BARTLEY (*working at the halter, to* **CATHLEEN**) Let you go down each day, and see the sheep aren't jumping in on the rye, and if the jobber comes you can sell the pig with the black feet if there is a good price going.

MAURYA How would the like of her get a good price for a pig?

BARTLEY (*to* CATHLEEN) If the west wind holds with the last bit of the moon let you and Nora get up weed enough for another cock for the kelp. It's hard set we'll be from this day with no one in it but one man to work.

MAURYA It's hard set we'll be surely the day you're drownd'd with the rest. What way will I live and the girls with me, and I an old woman looking for the grave?

[BARTLEY lays down the halter, takes off his old coat, and puts on a newer on of the same flannel.]

BARTLEY (*to* NORA) Is she coming to the pier?

NORA (*looking out*) She's passing the green head and letting fall her sails.

BARTLEY (*getting his purse and tobacco*) I'll have half an hour to go down, and you'll see me coming again in two days, or in three days, or maybe in four days if the wind is bad.

MAURYA (*turning round to the fire, and putting her shawl over her head*) Isn't it a hard and cruel man won't hear a word from an old woman, and she holding him from the sea?

CATHLEEN It's the life of a young man to be going on the sea, and who would listen to an old woman with one thing and she saying it over?

BARTLEY (*taking the halter*) I must go now quickly. I'll ride down on the red mare, and the gray pony'll run behind me. . . . The blessing of God on you.

[He goes out.]

MAURYA (*crying out as he is in the door*) He's gone now, God spare us, and we'll not see him again. He's gone now, and when the black night is falling I'll have no son left me in the world.

CATHLEEN Why wouldn't you give him your blessing and he looking round in the door? Isn't it sorrow enough is on every one in this house without your sending him out with an unlucky word behind him, and a hard word in his ear?

[MAURYA takes up the tongs and begins raking the fire aimlessly without looking around.]

NORA (*turning towards her*) You're taking away the turf from the cake.

CATHLEEN (*crying out*) The Son of God forgive us, Nora, we're after forgetting his bit of bread.

[She comes over to the fire.]

NORA And it's destroyed he'll be going till dark night, and he after eating nothing since the sun went up.

CATHLEEN (*turning the cake out of the oven*) It's destroyed he'll be, surely. There's no sense left on any person in a house where an old woman will be talking for ever.

[MAURYA sways herself on her stool.]

CATHLEEN (*cutting off some of the bread and rolling it in a cloth; to* **MAURYA**) Let you go down now to the spring well and give him this and he passing. You'll see him then and the dark word will be broken, and you can say, "God speed you," the way he'll be easy in his mind.

MAURYA (*taking the bread*) Will I be in it as soon as himself?

CATHLEEN If you go now quickly.

MAURYA (*standing up unsteadily*) It's hard set I am to walk.

CATHLEEN (looking at her anxiously) Give her the stick, Nora, or maybe she'll slip on the big stones.

NORA What stick?

CATHLEEN The stick Michael brought from Connemara.

MAURYA (*taking a stick* **NORA** *gives her*) In the big world the old people do be leaving things after them for their sons and children, but in this place it is the young men do be leaving things behind for them that do be old.

[*She goes out slowly.* **NORA** *goes over to the ladder.*]

CATHLEEN (*looking out*) She's gone now. Throw it down quickly, for the Lord knows when she'll be out of it again.

NORA (*getting the bundle from the loft*) The young priest said he'd be passing tomorrow, and we might go down and speak to him below if it's Michael's they are surely.

CATHLEEN (*taking the bundle*) Did he say what way they were found?

NORA (*coming down*) "There were two men," says he, "and they rowing round with poteen before the cocks crowed, and the oar of one of them caught the body, and they passing the black cliffs of the north."

CATHLEEN (*trying to open the bundle*) Give me a knife, Nora, the string's perished with the salt water, and there's a black knot on it you wouldn't loosen in a week.

NORA (*giving her a knife*) I've heard tell it was a long way to Donegal.

CATHLEEN *(cutting the string)* It is surely. There was a man in here a while ago—the man sold us that knife—and he said if you set off walking from the rocks beyond, it would be seven days you'd be in Donegal.

NORA And what time would a man take, and he floating?

[CATHLEEN opens the bundle and takes out a bit of a stocking. They look at them eagerly.]

CATHLEEN *(in a low voice)* The Lord spare us, Nora! isn't it a queer hard thing to say if it's his they are surely?

NORA I'll get his shirt off the hook the way we can put the one flannel on the other. *(She looks through some clothes hanging in the corner.)* It's not with them, Cathleen, and where will it be?

CATHLEEN I'm thinking Bartley put it on him in the morning, for his own shirt was heavy with the salt in it. *(pointing to the corner)* There's a bit of a sleeve was of the same stuff. Give me that and it will do.

[NORA brings it to her and they compare the flannel.]

CATHLEEN It's the same stuff, Nora; but if it is itself aren't there great rolls of it in the shops of Galway, and isn't it many another man may have a shirt of it as well as Michael himself?

NORA *(who has taken up the stocking and counted the stitches, crying out)* It's Michael, Cathleen, it's Michael; God spare his soul, and what will herself say when she hears this story, and Bartley on the sea?

CATHLEEN *(taking the stocking)* It's a plain stocking.

NORA It's the second one of the third pair I knitted, and I put up three score stitches, and I dropped four of them.

CATHLEEN (*counts the stitches*) It's that number is in it. (*crying out*) Ah, Nora, isn't it a bitter thing to think of him floating that way to the far north, and no one to keen him but the black hags that do be flying on the sea?

NORA (*swinging herself round, and throwing out her arms on the clothes*) And isn't it a pitiful thing when there is nothing left of a man who was a great rower and fisher, but a bit of an old shirt and a plain stocking?

CATHLEEN (*after an instant*) Tell me is herself coming, Nora? I hear a little sound on the path.

NORA (*looking out*) She is, Cathleen. She's coming up to the door.

CATHLEEN Put these things away before she'll come in. Maybe it's easier she'll be after giving her blessing to Bartley, and we won't let on we've heard anything the time he's on the sea.

NORA (*helping* **CATHLEEN** *to close the bundle*) We'll put them here in the corner.

[*They put them into a hold in the chimney corner.* **CATHLEEN** *goes back to the spinning-wheel.*]

NORA Will she see it was crying I was?

CATHLEEN Keep your back to the door the way the light'll not be on you.

[**NORA** *sits down at the chimney corner, with her back to the door.* **MAURYA** *comes in very slowly, without looking at the girls, and goes over to her stool at the other side of the fire. The cloth with the bread is still in her hand. The girls*

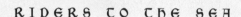

look at each other, and **NORA** *points to the bundle of bread.]*

CATHLEEN *(after spinning for a moment)* You didn't give him his bit of bread?

*[***MAURYA*** *begins to keen softly, without turning round.]*

CATHLEEN Did you see him riding down?

*[***MAURYA*** *goes on keening.]*

CATHLEEN *(a little impatiently)* God forgive you; isn't it a better thing to raise your voice and tell what you seen, than to be making lamentation for a thing that's done? Did you see Bartley, I'm saying to you.

MAURYA *(with a weak voice)* My heart's broken from this day.

CATHLEEN *(as before)* Did you see Bartley?

MAURYA I seen the fearfulest thing.

CATHLEEN *(leaves her wheel and looks out)* God forgive you; he's riding the mare now over the green head, and the gray pony behind him.

MAURYA *(starts, so that her shawl falls back from her head and shows her white tossed hair. With a frightened voice)* The gray pony behind him.

CATHLEEN *(coming to the fire)* What is it ails you, at all?

MAURYA *(speaking very slowly)* I've seen the fearfulest thing any person has seen, since the day Bride Dara seen the dead man with the child in his arms.

CATHLEEN and **NORA** Uah.

[They crouch down in front of the old woman at the fire.]

NORA Tell us what it is you seen.

MAURYA I went down to the spring

well, and I stood there saying a prayer to myself. Then Bartley came along, and he riding on the red mare with the gray pony behind him. *(She puts up her hands, as if to hide something from her eyes.)* The Son of God spare us, Nora!

CATHLEEN What is it you seen.

MAURYA I seen Michael himself.

CATHLEEN *(speaking softly)* You did not, mother; It wasn't Michael you seen, for his body is after being found in the far north, and he's got a clean burial by the grace of God.

MAURYA *(a little defiantly)* I'm after seeing him this day, and he riding and galloping. Bartley came first on the red mare; and I tried to say "God speed you," but something choked the words in my throat. He went by quickly; and "the blessing of God on you," says he, and I could say noth-ing. I looked up then, and I crying, at the gray pony, and there was Michael upon it—with fine clothes on him, and new shoes on his feet.

CATHLEEN *(begins to keen)* It's destroyed we are from this day. It's destroyed, surely.

NORA Didn't the young priest say the Almighty God wouldn't leave her destitute with no son living?

MAURYA *(in a low voice, but clearly)* It's little the like of him knows of the sea. . . . Bartley will be lost now, and let you call in Eamon and make me a good coffin out of the white boards, for I won't live after them. I've had a husband, and a husband's father, and six sons in this house—six fine men, though it was a hard birth I had with every one of them and they coming to the world—and some of them were found and some of them were not found, but they're gone now the lot of them. . . . There were Stephen, and Shawn, were lost in the great wind, and found after in the Bay of Gregory of the Golden Mouth, and carried up the two off them on the one plank, and in by that door.

[She pauses for a moment, the girls start as if they heard something through the door that is half open behind them.]

NORA *(in a whisper)* Did you hear that, Cathleen? Did you hear a noise in the north-east?

CATHLEEN *(in a whisper)* There's some one after crying out by the seashore.

MAURYA *(continues without hearing anything)* There was Sheamus and his father, and his own father again, were lost in a dark night, and not a stick or sign was seen of them when the sun went up. There was Patch after was drowned out of a curagh that turned over. I was sitting here with Bartley, and he a baby, lying on my two knees, and I seen two women, and three women, and four women coming in, and they crossing themselves, and not saying a word. I looked out then, and there were men coming after them, and they holding a thing in the half of a red sail, and water dripping out of it—it was a dry day, Nora—and leaving a track to the door.

[She pauses again with her hand stretched out towards the door. It opens softly and old women begin to come in, crossing themselves on the threshold, and kneeling down in front of the stage with red petticoats over their heads.]

MAURYA *(half in a dream, to* **CATHLEEN***)* Is it Patch, or Michael, or what is it at all?

CATHLEEN Michael is after being found in the far north, and when he is found there how could he be here in this place?

MAURYA There does be a power of young men floating round in the sea, and what way would they know if it was Michael they had, or another man like him, for when a man is nine days in the sea, and the wind blowing, it's hard set his own mother would be to say what man was it.

CATHLEEN It's Michael, God spare him, for they're after sending us a bit of his clothes from the far north.

[She reaches out and hands **MAURYA** *the clothes that belonged to Michael.* **MAURYA** *stands up slowly and takes them in her hands.* **NORA** *looks out.]*

NORA They're carrying a thing among them and there's water dripping out of it and leaving a track by the big stones.

CATHLEEN *(in a whisper to the women who have come in)* Is it Bartley it is?

ONE OF THE WOMEN It is surely, God rest his soul.

[Two younger women come in and pull out the table. Then men carry in the body of Bartley, laid on a plank, with a bit of a sail over it, and lay it on the table.]

CATHLEEN *(to the women, as they are doing so)* What way was he drowned?

ONE OF THE WOMEN The gray pony knocked him into the sea, and he was washed out where there is a great surf on the white rocks.

[**MAURYA** *has gone over and knelt down at the head of the table. The women are keening softly and swaying themselves with a slow movement.* **CATHLEEN** *and* **NORA** *kneel at the other end of the table. The men kneel near the door.*]

MAURYA (*raising her head and speaking as if she did not see the people around her*) They're all gone now, and there isn't anything more the sea can do to me. . . . I'll have no call now to be up crying and praying when the wind breaks from the south, and you can hear the surf is in the east, and the surf is in the west, making a great stir with the two noises, and they hitting one on the other. I'll have no call now to be going down and getting Holy Water in the dark nights after Samhain, and I won't care what way the sea is when the other women will be keening. (*To* **NORA**) Give me the Holy Water, Nora, there's a small sup still on the dresser.

[**NORA** *gives it to her.*]

MAURYA (*drops Michael's clothes across* **BARTLEY**'s *feet, and sprinkles the Holy Water over him*) It isn't that I haven't prayed for you, Bartley, to the Almighty God. It isn't that I haven't said prayers in the dark night til you wouldn't know what I'ld be saying; but it's a great rest I'll have now, and great sleeping in the long nights after Samhain, if it's only a bit of wet flour we do have to eat, and maybe a fish that would be stinking.

[*She kneels down again, crossing herself, and saying prayers under her breath.*]

CATHLEEN (*to an old man*) Maybe yourself and Eamon would make a

coffin when the sun rises. We have fine white boards herself bought, God help her, thinking Michael would be found, and I have a new cake you can eat while you'll be working.

THE OLD MAN (*looking at the boards*) Are there nails with them?

CATHLEEN There are not, Colum; we didn't think of the nails.

ANOTHER MAN It's a great wonder she wouldn't think of the nails, and all the coffins she's seen made already.

CATHLEEN It's getting old she is, and broken.

[MAURYA *stands up again very slowly and spreads out the pieces of Michael's clothes beside the body, sprinkling them with the last of the Holy Water.*]

NORA (*in a whisper to* **CATHLEEN**) She's quiet now and easy; but the day Michael was drowned you could hear her crying out from this to the spring well. It's fonder she was of Michael, and would any one have thought that?

CATHLEEN (*slowly and clearly*) An old woman will be soon tired with anything she will do, and isn't it nine days herself is after crying and keening, and making great sorrow in the house?

MAURYA (*puts the empty cup mouth downwards on the table, and lays her hands together on* **BARTLEY**'*s feet*) They're all together this time, and the end is come. May the Almighty God have mercy on Bartley's soul, and on Michael's soul, and on the souls of Sheamus and Patch, and Stephen and Shawn (bending her head); and may he have mercy on my soul, Nora, and

on the soul of every one is left living in the world.

[She pauses, and the keen rises a little more loudly from the women, then sinks away.]

MAURYA *(continuing)* Michael has a clean burial in the far north, by the grace of the Almighty God. Bartley will have a fine coffin out of the white boards, and a deep grave surely. What more can we want than that? No man at all can be living for ever, and we must be satisfied.

[She kneels down again and the curtain falls slowly.]. ●

JOHN MILLINGTON SYNGE (pronounced *sing*) (1871–1909) was born to a Protestant family of the professional classes and acquired a diverse cultural education (violin in Germany, literature in Paris, and fluency in Hebrew, German, French, and Irish) as well as a degree from Trinity College, Dublin. His works prominently featured the peasantry of western Ireland and the Aran Islands—in particular his travel memoir *The Aran Islands*. He produced other essays, translations, and poetry, but found his greatest success in drama with such plays as *In the Shadow of the Glen* (1903) and the controversial *The Playboy of the Western World* (1907). This play, *Riders to the Sea* (1904), is considered by many the "only one-act tragedy in the English language."

The Song of
Wandering Aengus

by W.B. Yeats

I WENT out to the hazel wood,
Because a fire was in my head,
And cut and peeled a hazel wand,
And hooked a berry to a thread;
And when white moths were on
     the wing,
And moth-like stars were
     flickering out,
I dropped the berry in a stream
And caught a little silver trout.

When I had laid it on the floor
I went to blow the fire a-flame,
But something rustled on
     the floor,
And someone called me by
     my name:
It had become a glimmering girl

With apple blossom in her hair
Who called me by my name
     and ran
And faded through the
     brightening air.

Though I am old with wandering
Through hollow lands and hilly
     lands,
I will find out where she has gone,
And kiss her lips and take
     her hands;
And walk among long dappled
     grass,
And pluck till time and times
     are done,
The silver apples of the moon,
The golden apples of the sun.

The Croppy Boy

It was early, early in the spring
The birds did whistle and sweetly sing
Changing their notes from tree to tree
And the song they sang was Old Ireland free.

It was early, early in the night,
The yeoman cavalry gave me a fright
The yeoman cavalry was my downfall
And I was taken by Lord Cornwall.

'Twas in the guard-house where I was laid,
And in a parlour where I was tried
My sentence passed and my courage low
When to Dungannon I was forced to go.

As I was passing my father's door
My brother William stood at the door
My aged father stood at the door
And my tender mother her hair she tore.

As I was going up Wexford Street
My own first cousin I chanced to meet;
My own first cousin did me betray
And for one bare guinea swore
    my life away.

As I was walking up Wexford Hill
Who could blame me to cry my fill?
I looked behind, and I looked before
But my aged mother I shall see
    no more.

And as I mounted the platform high
My aged father was standing by;
My aged father did me deny
And the name he gave me was
    the Croppy Boy.

It was in Dungannon this young
    man died
And in Dungannon his body lies.
And you good people that do pass by
Oh shed a tear for the Croppy Boy.

STEAK AND GUINNESS PIE

This is the perfect antidote to the wet and windy weather Ireland is famous for. If you can't be with friends in a cozy pub with the fire going—and a brilliant fiddler playing a tune—cook this up at home on a winter's night, put on a Christy Moore CD, and invite someone Irish to dinner.

8 slices bacon
2 pounds round steaks
1 tablespoon flour (seasoned with a
    pinch of salt and pepper)
5 onions, peeled and chopped
$1/3$ cup raisins (optional)
1 cup peas
2–3 tablespoons chopped parsley
1 teaspoon brown sugar
$1^1/3$ cups Guinness stout
1 sheet puff pastry
Oil

1. Brown the bacon in a frying pan. Remove from the pan. When it's cool, crumble it into small pieces.
2. Cut the steaks into bite-size cubes, roll in the flour mixture, and brown in the bacon drippings, adding extra oil if necessary. When browned, place the meat and crumbled bacon in a covered casserole dish.
3. Sauté the onions in the drippings/oil until golden, then add them to the meat. Add the raisins, peas, parsley, brown sugar, and Guinness, cover tightly, and simmer over low heat or in a very moderate oven (325° to 350° F) for 2 to $2^1/2$ hours. Stir occasionally, and add more Guinness or water if the gravy gets too thick.
4. Roll out the pastry to fit the casserole. Place it on top of the meat mixture and bake according to package directions or until puffed golden.

Yield: 8 servings.

Sláinte!

(health!)

IRISH TOASTS!

Here's to you as good as you are,
And to me as bad as I am;
I'm as good as you are,
Bad and all as I am.

Oh Mother dear, I'm over here
and I'm never coming back.
What keeps me here is the beer,
the women, and the craic!

Thirst begets thirst
So be getting yours first;
Good luck! Stay sane!
Down the dusty lane!

The man whose pocket and purse are empty
He cannot pay like the other men,
Let this man here pay for that man there
And God will pay for the last man then.

IRISH TOASTS!

For every wound, a balm.
For every sorrow, a cheer.
For every storm, a calm.
For every thirst, a beer.

❧

May we always have a clean shirt, a clear
conscience, and a few bob in our pockets.
Or if not, a decent man to stand us a drink!

❧

Here's to cheating, stealing, fighting, and drinking.
If you cheat, may you cheat death.
If you steal, may you steal a woman's heart.
If you fight, may you fight for a brother.
And if you drink, may you drink with me.

❧

When money's tight and hard to get
and your horse is also-ran,
When all you have is a heap of debt
a pint of plain is your only man.

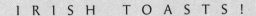

IRISH TOASTS!

Wet your whistle well and
may we never die of the drought!

Here's to good Irish friends
Never above you
Never below you
Always beside you
Health to the man who buys his round
To heaven's alehouse be he bound.

At the end of the day,
Let us drink to work well done,
And if you are an idler,
We'll toast tomorrow's fun.

Here's to good Irish friends

May the roof above us never fall in
And may us good companions beneath it
Never fall out.

FACTS & FANCY
PUB HOPPING

"**A**good puzzle would be to cross Dublin without passing a pub," James Joyce is supposed to have said, and that pretty much sums up the situation in the entire country. The Irish pub is not a bar in the American sense: a hangout for the young and single (or the old and lonely). No, it's more like a Parisian café. A place where friends and family—of all ages and across all social strata—meet, eat (panini nowadays as likely as bangers and mash), listen to live music, and, most of all, gab. Regulars sit with a drink (or two) for hours at their "local," and sooner or later everyone *and* their Aunt Mae will pass through with an amusing tale or two concerning the news of the day. That's not to say that drinking is ignored—not by a long shot—but the corner pub is more about social interaction and a bit of *craic*, two necessities of Irish life.

PUB 101

* Order by pint or glass (a glass is a half pint); men rarely order a glass.

* Do not order an appletini—pubs are not big on mixed drinks in general. Even when ordering something as simple as a gin and tonic, don't be surprised if the gin comes in one glass and the tonic in another.

* To meet a regular, park yourself at the bar.

  * If you want more privacy, sit in a "snug" (one of those cute booths).

* Tipping is done by buying the bartender a drink along with your order (leaving cash on the bar is uncommon).

* Hours vary slightly depending on the day, but generally 10:30 a.m. to 11:30 p.m.; if loads of fun is still being had at closing, publicans have been known to lock the doors with the punters still inside (not that it's legal).

* Everyone is expected to have (and give) an opinion (on anything . . . and everything).

What's on Tap

* Guinness, a thick and creamy stout; try it—it's better in Ireland; notice how long it takes to pour

* Smithwicks, a light red ale—pronounced "Smith-Icks" or in deepest Dublin, "Smiddicks"

* Beamish, a less-famous stout

* Harp, an Irish lager

* Murphy's, another stout and Guinness's main competitor

* Kilkenny, an ale similar to Smithwicks

* Caffrey's, an ale from Belfast

The Oldest Pub in Ireland

Surprise! There is much dispute about a simple question of fact: Which is the oldest pub in the country? Grace Neill's in Donaghadee, County Down, received its license in 1611. Its Web site proclaims, "Grace Neill's is the oldest pub in Ireland." And they have a ghost. But the Brazen Head in Dublin claims that it has been a pub since 1198. (Prior to that—meaning in the days of the Norman invasion—it was only a coach inn.) And last, there's Sean's Pub in Athlone, County Westmeath, which claims to "almost certainly" be the oldest pub in the *world*. According to the *Guinness Book of World Records*, 2004 (who else could decide such a thing?), Sean's Pub is the oldest—but only by a drop!

Whiskey in the Jar

As I went out a-walking on the far-flung Kerry mountains,
I met with Captain Everett and his money he was counting,
I first took out my pistol and I then took out my rapier,
Saying 'Stand and deliver, for you are my bold deceiver.'

Chorus
Whack faddle daddy-O,
Whack faddle daddy-O,
There's whiskey in the jar. (Repeat)

I counted out his money and it made a pretty penny,
I'll take it off and give it to my bonny, sporting Jenny.
She sighed and she swore and she said she'd ne'er betray me,
But the devil take the women for they never can be easy.

Chorus

294

I went up to my chamber all for to take a slumber,
I dreamt of gold and jewels, and sure it was no wonder,
For Jenny drew my charges and she filled them up with water,
And sent for Captain Everett to be ready for the slaughter.

Chorus

It was early in the morning between six o'clock and seven,
Up rode a band of footmen and likewise Captain Everett,
I first produced my pistol for she'd stolen away my rapier,
But I couldn't shoot the water so a prisoner I was taken.

Chorus

There's only one to help me now,
    'tis my brother in the army,
But I don't know where he's stationed,
    be it Cork or in Killarney.
But if he comes to free me we'll go
    wandering in Kilkenny,
I'll engage he'll treat me better than
    my darling, sporting Jenny.

Chorus

Deirdre and Naoise

*Long ago in ancient Ireland, a baby girl named Deirdre was born to Feidhlim, the
court harper to King Conchubar of Ulster. The druid Cathbad prophesized that the
child would become the most beautiful girl in Ireland. The prophecy became true, and
when she came of age King Conchubar desired Deirdre for his wife. While promised
to the king, Deirdre met the Sons of Usnach and fell in love with Naoise, the bravest
of the brothers. King Conchubar would not relinquish his bride-to-be and murdered
Naoise. In sorrow, Deirdre took her own life. In this passage by Lady Gregory,
Deirdre and Naoise meet for the first time.*

One day Deirdre and her companions were out on a hill near
Emain Macha, looking around them in the pleasant sunshine, and they saw three men walking together. Deirdre
was looking at the men and wondering at them, and when
they came near, she remembered the talk of the hunter, and the three men
she saw in her dream, and she thought to herself that these were the three
sons of Usnach, and that this was Naoise, that had his head and shoulders
above all the men of Ireland. The three brothers went by without turning

Deirdre and Naoise

their eyes at all upon the young girls on the hillside, and they were singing as they went, and whoever heard the low singing of the sons of Usnach, it was enchantment and music to them, and every cow that was being milked and heard it, gave two-thirds more of milk. And it is what happened, that love for Naoise came into the heart of Deirdre, so that she could not but follow him. She gathered up her skirt and went after the three men that had gone past the foot of the hill, leaving her companions there after her.

But Ainnle and Ardan had heard talk of the young girl that was at Conchubar's Court, and it is what they thought, that if Naoise their brother would see her, it is for himself he would have her, for she was not yet married to the king. So when they saw Deirdre coming after them, they said to one another to hasten their steps, for they had a long road to travel, and the dusk of night coming on. They did so, and Deirdre saw it, and she cried out after them, "Naoise, son of Usnach, are you going to leave me?" "What cry was that came to my ears, that it is not well for me to answer, and not easy for me to refuse?" said Naoise. "It was nothing but the cry of Conchubar's wild ducks," said his brothers; "but let us quicken our steps and hasten our feet, for we have a long road to travel,

Deirdre and Naoise

and the dusk of the evening coming on." They did so, and were widening the distance between themselves and her. Then Deirdre cried, "Naoise! Naoise! son of Usnach, are you going to leave me?" "What cry was it that came to my ears and struck my heart, that it is not well for me to answer, or easy for me to refuse?" said Naoise. "Nothing but the cry of Conchubar's wild geese," said his brothers; "but let us quicken our steps and hasten our feet, the darkness of night is coming on." They did so and were widening the distance between themselves and her. Then Deirdre cried the third time, "Naoise! Naoise! Naoise! son of Usnach, are you going to leave me?" "What sharp, clear cry was that, the sweetest that ever came to my ears, and the sharpest that ever struck my heart, of all the cries I ever heard," said Naoise. "What is it but the scream of Conchubar's lake swans," said his brothers. "That was the third cry of some person beyond there," said Naoise, "and I swear by my hand of valor," he said, "I will go no further until I see where the cry comes from." So Naoise turned back and met Deirdre, and Deirdre and Naoise kissed one another three times, and she gave a kiss to each of his brothers. And with the confusion that was on her, a blaze of red fire came upon her, and her color came and went as quickly as the aspen by the stream. And it is

Deirdre and Naoise

what Naoise thought to himself, that he never saw a woman so beautiful in his life; and he gave Deirdre, there and then, the love that he never gave to living thing, to vision, or to creature, but to herself alone.

FACTS & FANCY
IRELAND'S KING

Patsy Dan Rodgers is his name and, according to him he "seems to be" the only king in the country. While not king *of* the country, he does reign over tiny Tory Island, which is about nine miles north of Donegal and can be reached, weather permitting, by daily ferry.

For the past 1,400 years every generation has "by consensus" agreed on a king of Tory Island. He does not answer to anyone, including the Taoiseach (prime minister), the Irish Parliament, or the president. His duties do, however, include welcoming visitors to the kingdom of around 170 souls, giving guided tours, and "singing the odd song." His Majesty's talents also include painting (he exhibited in New York in 2005), dancing, and playing the button-key accordion. Gaelic, he says, is his first language, but he has an excellent grasp of—and charming way with—English. ❦

Advice to a Prince

The kings of the Irish provinces met to appoint a High King of the land, for the country had been without one for many years. The kings made a bull-feast and waited for the word of a dreamer to guide them to their new leader. The dreamer screamed out in his sleep of a man with red stripes sitting over a dying man in Ulster. The dying man was the legendary Cuchulain. When Cuchulain heard this, he rose up in his weakness and addressed Lugaid of the Red Stripes, the future King of Ireland, with this advice in this passage by Lady Gregory.

"**D**o not be a frightened man in a battle; do not be light-minded, hard to reach, or proud. Do not be ungentle, or hasty, or passionate; do not be overcome with the drunkenness of great riches, like a flea that is drowned in the ale of a king's house. Do not scatter many feasts to strangers; do not visit mean people that cannot receive you as a king. Do not let wrongful possession stand because it has lasted long, but let witnesses be searched to know who is the right owner of land. Let the tellers of history tell truth before you; let the lands of brothers and their increase be set down in their lifetime; if a family has increased in its branches, is it not from the

one stem they are come? Let them be called up, let the old claims be established by oaths; let the heir be left in lawful possession of the place his fathers lived in; let strangers be driven off it by force.

"Do not use too many words. Do not speak noisily; do not mock, do not give insults, do not make little of old people. Do not think ill of any one; do not ask what is hard to give. Let you have a law of lending, a law of oppression, a law of pledging. Be obedient to the advice of the wise; keep in mind the advice of the old. Be a follower of the rules of your fathers. Do not be cold-hearted to friends; be strong towards your enemies; do not give evil for evil in your battles. Do not be given to too much talking. Do not speak any harm of others. Do not waste, do not scatter, do not do away with what is your own. When you do wrong, take the blame of it; do not give up the truth for any man. Do not be trying to be first, the way you will not be jealous; do not be an idler, that you may not be weak; do not ask too much, that you may not be thought little of. Are you willing to follow this advice, my son?"

Then Lugaid answered Cuchulain, and it is what he said: "As long as all goes well, I will keep to your words, and every one will know that there is nothing wanting in me; all will be done that can be done."

Then Lugaid went away with the messengers to Teamhair, and he was made king, and he slept in Teamhair that night. And after that all the people that had gathered there went to their own homes.

Old Ireland

by Walt Whitman

Far hence amid an isle of wondrous beauty,
Crouching over a grave an ancient sorrowful mother,
Once a queen, now lean and tatter'd seated on the ground,
Her old white hair drooping dishvel'd round her shoulders,
At her feet fallen an unused royal harp,
Long silent, she too long silent, mourning her shrouded hope and heir,
Of all the earth her heart most full of sorrow because most full of love.
Yet a word ancient mother,
You need crouch there no longer on the cold ground with
        forehead between your knees,
O you need not sit there veil'd in your old white hair so dishevel'd,
For know you the one you mourn is not in that grave,
It was an illusion, the son you love was not really dead,
The Lord is not dead, he is risen again young and strong in
        another country,
Even while you wept there by your fallen harp by the grave,
What you wept for was translated, pass'd from the grave,
The winds favor'd and the sea sail'd it,
And now with rosy and new blood,
Moves to-day in a new country.

THE HUNGRY DEATH

BY ROSA MULHOLLAND

All through that summer the rain fell, and, when autumn came in Bofin, there was no harvest either of fuel or of food. The potato-seed had been for the most part washed out of the earth without putting forth a shoot, while those that remained in the ground were nearly rotted by a loathsome disease. The smiling little fields that grew the food were turned into blackened pits, giving forth a horrid stench. Winter was beginning again, the year having been but one long winter, with seas too wild to be often braved by even the sturdiest of the fishermen, and the fish seeming to have deserted the island. Accustomed to exist on what would satisfy no other race, and to trust cheerfully to Providence to send them that little out of the earth and out of the sea, the people bore up cheerfully for a long time, living on a mess of Indian-meal once a day, mingled with such edible sea-weed as they could gather off the rocks. So long as shopkeepers in Galway and other towns could afford to give credit to the island, the hooker kept bringing such scanty supplies as were now the sole sustenance of the impoverished population. But credit began to fail, and universal distress on the mainland gave back an answering wail to the hunger-cry of the Bofiners. It is hard for anyone who has never witnessed such a state of things to imagine the condition of ten or twelve hundred living creatures on a barren island girded round with angry breakers; the strong arms around them paralyzed, first by the storms that dash their boats to pieces, and rend and destroy their fishing gear, and the devastation of the earth that makes labor useless, and later by the faintness and sickness which comes from hunger long endured, and the cold from which they have no longer a defense. Accustomed as they are to the hardships of recurring years of trial, the Bofiners became gradually aware that a visitation was at hand for which there had seldom been a parallel. Earth and sea alike barren and pitiless to their needs, whence could deliverance come unless the heavens rained down manna into their mouths? Alas! no miracle was wrought, and after a term of brave struggle, laughter, music, song faded out of the island; feet that had danced as long as it was possible now might hardly walk, and the weakest among the people began to die. Troops of children that a few months ago were rosy and sturdy, sporting on the sea-shore, now stretched their emaciated limbs by the fireless hearths, and wasted to death before their maddened mothers' eyes. The old and ailing vanished like flax before a flame. Digging of graves was soon the chief labor of the island, and a day seemed near at hand when the survivors would no longer have strength to perform even this last service for the dead.

ROSA MULHOLLAND (1841–1921) was determined to be a painter, but soon met Charles Dickens who convinced her to pursue writing. He published her story "Not to Be Taken at Bed-time" and wrote "To Be Taken with a Grain of Salt" as a companion piece.

FACTS & FANCY
AN GORTA MÓR

The Great Famine, commonly known outside Ireland as the Irish Potato Famine, nearly destroyed the whole of the population in Ireland between 1845 and 1851. The famine was at least 50 years in the making due to the disastrous combination of British economic policies (particularly the Property Act, which forbade Irish Catholics to pass the family landholdings on to a single son), destructive farming methods, and the unfortunate appearance of "the Blight," a potato fungus that quickly spread across Europe and destroyed the primary food source for the majority of the Irish population. The number of deaths is unrecorded, but estimates suggest that somewhere between 500,000 and more than 1 million perished in the five years from 1846. Approximately two million refugees fled to all corners of the world, including Great Britain, the Americas, and Australia, in the aftermath. In the United States, in particular, most Irish immigrants traveled to the major cities and settled where they landed, unable to afford further travel. In little time, the Irish made up a quarter of the population of several cities, including Boston, New York City, and Philadelphia, and they continue to shape their character today. *

Digging by Seamus Heaney

Between my finger and my thumb
The squat pen rests; snug as a gun.

Under my window, a clean rasping sound
When the spade sinks into gravelly ground:
My father, digging. I look down

Till his straining rump among the flowerbeds
Bends low, comes up twenty years away
Stooping in rhythm through potato drills
Where he was digging.

The coarse boot nestled on the lug, the shaft
Against the inside knee was levered firmly.
He rooted out tall tops, buried the bright
    edge deep
To scatter new potatoes that we picked
Loving their cool hardness in our hands.

By God, the old man could handle a spade.
Just like his old man.

My grandfather cut more turf in a day
Than any other man on Toner's bog.
Once I carried him milk in a bottle
Corked sloppily with paper. He straightened up
To drink it, then fell to right away

Nicking and slicing neatly, heaving sods
Over his shoulder, going down and down
For the good turf. Digging.

The cold smell of potato mould, the squelch and slap
Of soggy peat, the curt cuts of an edge
Through living roots awaken in my head.
But I've no spade to follow men like them.

Between my finger and my thumb
The squat pen rests.
I'll dig with it.

Over in Killarney,
Many years ago,
Me Mither sang a song to me
In tones so sweet and low,
Just a simple little ditty,
In her good ould Irish way,
And I'd give the world if she could sing
That song to me this day.

Chorus
"Too-ra-loo-ra-loo-ral, Too-ra-loo-ra-li,
Too-ra-loo-ra-loo-ral, Hush now, don't you cry!
Too-ra-loo-ra-loo-ral, Too-ra-loo-ra-loo-ri,
Too-ra-loo-ra-loo-ral, That's an Irish lullaby."

Oft, in dreams, I wander
To that cot again,
I feel her arms a-huggin' me
As when she held me then.
And I hear her voice a-hummin'
To me as in days of yore,
When she used to rock me fast asleep
Outside the cabin door.

Chorus

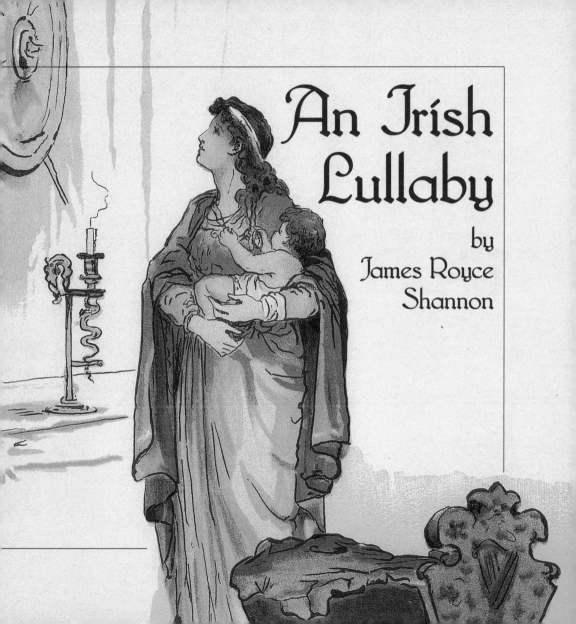

An Irish Lullaby

by
James Royce Shannon

Fiddlers & Storytellers

Before the written word arrived in Ireland, stories of giants, heroes, kings, and fairies were told and retold over the millennia by a seanachai (pronounced shanaky), or storyteller. As one theory goes, cultures that rely on the spoken word to keep history and culture alive often use rhyme or music to help remember the tales. Whether this is true about the Irish or not, there's no denying that there is an extraordinary amount of talented Irish storytellers and musicians. Here are a few.

ALTAN: Traditional ☘ ANUNA: Choral group, traditional, and Medieval ☘ MARY BLACK: Contemporary and traditional vocalist ☘ THE BOTHY BAND: Seventies new Irish traditional ☘ MAIRE BREATNACH: Fiddle player ☘ KARAN CASEY: Singer/songwriter ☘ THE CHIEFTAINS: Traditional ☘ CLANNAD: Traditional ☘ THE CORRS: Traditional pop band ☘ THE CRANBERRIES: Pop rock band ☘ DANU: Traditional ☘ THE DUBLINERS: Legendary folk group ☘ ENYA: Composer/vocalist ☘ RORY GALLAGHER: Rock ☘ JAMES GALWAY: Flutist ☘ GRÁINNE HAMBLY: Harper ☘ THE IRISH ROVERS: Legendary folk group ☘ THE JIVENAIRES: Sixties showband ☘ CATHY JORDAN: Traditional vocalist ☘ DOLORES KEANE: Galway singer ☘ KILA: "Alternative" traditional ☘ JOSEPH LOCKE: Irish tenor ☘ SINÉAD LOHAN: Singer/songwriter ☘ MAKEM & CLANCY: Legendary folk balladeers ☘ JOSEPHINE MARSH: Accordionist ☘ ELEANOR McEVOY: Vocalist ☘ ÁINE MINOGUE: Vocalist, harper ☘ CHRISTY MOORE: Traditional ☘ VAN MORRISON: World-renown singer/songwriter ☘ SINÉAD O'CONNOR: Vocalist ☘ MÍCHEÁL Ó SUILLEABHÁIN: Contemporary composer, instrumentalist ☘ FRANK PATTERSON: Irish tenor ☘ TOMMY PEOPLES: Fiddle legend ☘ THE POGUES: Rock ☘ THE SAWDOCTORS: Farmer-rock from the midlands ☘ THE SICK AND INDIGENT SONG CLUB: Blues and traditional (Monday nights at the Ha'penny Bridge Inn, Dublin) ☘ SOLAS: Traditional ☘ JOHN SPILLANE: Popular singer/songwriter ☘ U2: rock band ☘ JOHN WHELAN: Accordionist ☘ GER WOLFE: Popular singer/songwriter

WILD BLACKBERRY PIE

On a recent biking trip through the Mountains of Mourne (see page 28), there were two things that stopped me in my tracks. The first was a trio of wild horses—one white, one black, one roan—that came galloping toward me as I was pedaling along a country road. And the second was the abundant, wild, and luscious blackberries that just grew—to a New Yorker—like black diamonds from the bushes all along the route. I couldn't possibly pass by without a taste.

1 9-inch double-crust pie pastry
4 cups fresh blackberries
3 tablespoons whole wheat pastry
    flour
1 cup sugar or sucanat
1 tablespoon lemon juice
1 teaspoon lemon zest
1 teaspoon ground cinnamon
2 tablespoons butter

1. Preheat the oven to 450° F.
2. Line a 9-inch pie pan with half the pastry. Save the remaining pastry for the top crust. Chill both while preparing the blackberries.
3. Combine the berries, flour, sugar, lemon juice, lemon zest, and cinnamon. Pour into the pie shell and dot with butter. Cover with the top crust, and slash in several places.
4. Bake for 15 minutes. Reduce the heat to 350° F. Continue baking for 35 to 40 minutes, or until browned.

Yield: 1 pie.

Swans Mating

By Michael Longley

Even now I wish that you had been there
Sitting beside me on the riverbank:
The cob and his pen sailing in rhythm
Until their small heads met and the final
Heraldic moment dissolved in ripples.

The Piper and the Púca*

by Douglas Hyde

In the old times, there was a half fool living in Dunmore, in the county Galway, and although he was excessively fond of music, he was unable to learn more than one tune, and that was the "Black Rogue." He used to get a good deal of money from the gentlemen, for they used to get sport out of him. One night the piper was coming home from a house where there had been a dance, and he half drunk. When he came to a little bridge that was up by his mother's house, he squeezed the pipes on, and began playing the "Black Rogue" (*an rógaire dubh*). The Púca came behind him, and flung him up on his own back. There were long horns on the Púca, and the piper got a good grip of them, and then he said—

"Destruction on you, you nasty beast, let me home. I have a ten-penny piece in my pocket for my mother, and she wants snuff."

The Pooka, or Púca, seems essentially an animal spirit. Some derive his name from poc, a he-goat; and speculative persons consider him the forefather of Shakespeare's "Puck."

Myths & Folk Tales

The Piper and the Púca

"Never mind your mother," said the Púca, "but keep your hold. If you fall, you will break your neck and your pipes." Then the Púca said to him, "Play up for me the 'Shan Van Vocht' (*an t-seann-bhean bhocht*)."

"I don't know it," said the piper.

"Never mind whether you do or you don't," said the Púca. "Play up, and I'll make you know."

The piper put wind in his bag, and he played such music as made himself wonder.

"Upon my word, you're a fine music-master," says the piper then; "but tell me where you're for bringing me."

"There's a great feast in the house of the Banshee, on the top of Croagh Patric tonight," says the Púca, "and I'm for bringing you there to play music, and, take my word, you'll get the price of your trouble."

"By my word, you'll save me a journey, then," says the piper, "for Father William put a journey to Croagh Patric on me, because I stole the white gander from him last Martinmas."

The Púca rushed him across hills and bogs and rough places,

The Piper and the Púca

till he brought him to the top of Croagh Patric. Then the Púca struck three blows with his foot, and a great door opened, and they passed in together, into a fine room.

The piper saw a golden table in the middle of the room, and hundreds of old women (*cailleacha*) sitting round about it. The old women rose up, and said, "A hundred thousand welcomes to you, you Púca of November (*na Samhna*). Who is this you have with you?"

"The best piper in Ireland," says the Púca.

One of the old women struck a blow on the ground, and a door opened in the side of the wall, and what should the piper see coming out but the white gander which he had stolen from Father William.

"By my conscience, then," says the piper, "myself and my mother ate every taste of that gander, only one wing, and I gave that to Moy-rua (Red Mary), and it's she told the priest I stole the gander."

The gander cleaned the table, and carried it away, and the Púca said, "Play up music for these ladies."

The Piper and the Púca

The piper played up, and the old women began dancing, and they were dancing till they were tired. Then the Púca said to pay the piper, and every old woman drew out a gold piece, and gave it to him.

"By the tooth of Patric," said he, "I'm as rich as the son of a lord."

"Come with me," says the Púca, "and I'll bring you home."

They went out then, and just as he was going to ride on the Púca, the gander came up to him, and gave him a new set of pipes. The Púca was not long until he brought him to Dunmore, and he threw the piper off at the little bridge, and then he told him to go home, and says to him, "You have two things now that you never had before—you have sense and music" (*ciall agus ceól*).

The piper went home, and he knocked at his mother's door, saying, "Let me in, I'm as rich as a lord, and I'm the best piper in Ireland."

"You're drunk," said the mother.

"No, indeed," says the piper, "I haven't drunk a drop."

The Piper and the Púca

The mother let him in, and he gave her the gold pieces, and, "Wait now," says he, "till you hear the music I'll play."

He buckled on the pipes, but instead of music, there came a sound as if all the geese and ganders in Ireland were screeching together. He wakened the neighbors, and they were all mocking him, until he put on the old pipes, and then he played melodious music for them; and after that he told them all he had gone through that night.

The next morning, when his mother went to look at the gold pieces, there was nothing there but the leaves of a plant.

The piper went to the priest, and told him his story but the priest would not believe a word from him, until he put the pipes on him, and then the screeching of the ganders and geese began.

"Leave my sight, you thief," says the priest.

But nothing would do the piper till he would put the old pipes on him to show the priest that his story was true.

He buckled on the old pipes, and he played melodious music, and from that day till the day of his death, there was never a piper in the county Galway was as good as he was.

ANGELA'S ASHES

BY FRANK MCCOURT

Grandma sleeps in a big bed upstairs with a picture of the Sacred Heart of Jesus over her head and a statue of the Sacred Heart on the mantelpiece. She wants to switch from gaslight to electric light someday so that she'll have a little red light under the statue forever. Her devotion to the Sacred Heart is known up and down the lane and in lanes beyond.

Uncle Pat sleeps in a small bed in a corner of the same room where Grandma can make sure he comes in at a proper hour and kneels by the bed to say his prayers. He might have been dropped on his head, he may not know how to read and write, he may drink one pint too many, but there's no excuse for not saying his prayers before he goes to sleep.

Uncle Pat tells Grandma he met a man who is looking for place to stay that will let him wash himself morning and night and give him two meals a day, dinner and tea. His name is Bill Galvin and he has a good job down at the lime kiln. He's covered all the time with white lime dust but surely that's better than coal dust.

Grandma will have to give up her bed and move into the small room. She'll take the Sacred Heart picture and leave the statue to watch over the men. Besides, she has no place for a statue in her little room.

Bill Galvin comes after work to see the place. He's small, all white, and he

snuffles like a dog. He asks Grandma if she'd mind taking down that statue because he's a Protestant and he wouldn't be able to sleep. Grandma barks at Uncle Pat for not telling her he was dragging a Protestant into the house. Jesus, she says, there will be gossip up and down the lane and beyond.

Uncle Pat says he didn't know Bill Galvin was a Protestant. You could never tell by looking at him especially the way he's covered with lime. He looks like an ordinary Catholic and you'd never imagine a Protestant would be shoveling lime.

Bill Galvin says his poor wife that just died was a Catholic and she had the walls covered with pictures of the Sacred Heart and the Virgin Mary showing their hearts. He's not against the Sacred Heart himself, it's just that seeing the statue will remind him of his poor wife and give him the heartache.

Grandma says, Ah, God help us, why didn't you tell me that in the first place? Sure I can put the statue on the windowsill in my room and your heart won't be tormented at the sight of it.

Every morning Grandma cooks Bill's dinner and takes it to him at the lime kiln. Mam wonders why he can't take it with him in the morning and Grandma says, Do you expect me to get up at dawn and boil cabbage and pig's toes for his lordship to take in his dinner can?

Mam tells her, In another week school will be over and if you give Frank a sixpence a week he'll surely be glad to take Bill Galvin his dinner.

I don't want to go to Grandma's every day. I don't want to take Bill Galvin his

dinner all the way down the Dock Road, but Mam says that's sixpence we could use and if I don't do it I'm going nowhere else.

You're staying in the house, she says. You're not playing with your pals.

Grandma warns me to take the dinner can directly and not be meandering, looking this way and that, kicking canisters and ruining the toes of my shoes. This dinner is hot and that's the way Bill Galvin wants it.

There's a lovely smell from the dinner can, boiled bacon and cabbage and two big floury white potatoes. Surely he won't notice if I try half a potato. He won't complain to Grandma because he hardly ever talks outside of a snuffle or two.

It's better if I eat the other half potato so that he won't be asking why he got a half. I might as well try the bacon and cabbage too and if I eat the other potato he'll surely think she didn't send one at all.

The second potato melts in my mouth and I'll have to try another bit of cabbage, another morsel of bacon. There isn't much left now and he'll be very suspicious so I might as well finish off the rest.

What am I going to do now? Grandma will destroy me, Mam will keep me in for a year. Bill Galvin will bury me in lime. I'll tell him I was attacked by a dog on the Dock Road and he ate the whole dinner and I'm lucky I escaped without being eaten myself.

Oh, is that so? says Bill Galvin. And what's that bit of cabbage hanging on your gansey? Did the dog lick you wit his cabbagey gob? Go home and tell your

grandmother you ate me whole dinner and I'm falling down with the hunger here in this lime kiln.

She'll kill me.

Tell her don't kill you till she sends me some class of a dinner and if you don't go to her now and get me a dinner I'll kill you and throw your body into the lime there and there won't be much left for your mother to moan over.

Grandma says, What are you doin' back with that can? He could bring that back by himself.

He wants more dinner.

What do you mean more dinner? Jesus above, is it a hole he has in his leg?

He's falling down with the hunger below in the lime kiln.

Is it coddin' me you are?

He says send him any class of a dinner.

I will not. I sent him his dinner.

He didn't get it.

He didn't? Why not?

I ate it.

What?

ANGELA'S ASHES

I was hungry and I tasted it and I couldn't stop.

Jesus, Mary and holy St. Joseph.

She gives me a clout on the head that brings tears to my eyes. She screams at me like a banshee and jumps around the kitchen and threatens to drag me to the priest, the bishop, the Pope himself if he lived around the corner. She cuts bread and waves the knife at me and makes sandwiches of brawn and cold potatoes.

Take these sandwiches to Bill Galvin and if you even look cross-eyed at them I'll skin your hide.

Of course she runs to Mam and they agree the only way I can make up for my terrible sin is to deliver Bill Galvin's dinner for a fortnight without pay. I'm to bring back the can every day and that means I have to sit watching him stuff the food into his gob and he's not one that would ever ask you if you had a mouth in your head.

Every day I take the can back Grandma makes me kneel to the statue of the Sacred Heart and tell Him I'm sorry and all this over Bill Galvin, a Protestant. ●

FRANK McCOURT (1930–). The Pulitzer Prize–winning McCourt was born in Brooklyn, New York. He moved back to Ireland with his family at age 4 to live a magically miserable childhood before returning to New York at age 19. Teaching in New York City high schools for most of his life, he wrote his first book at an age most people would be retiring.

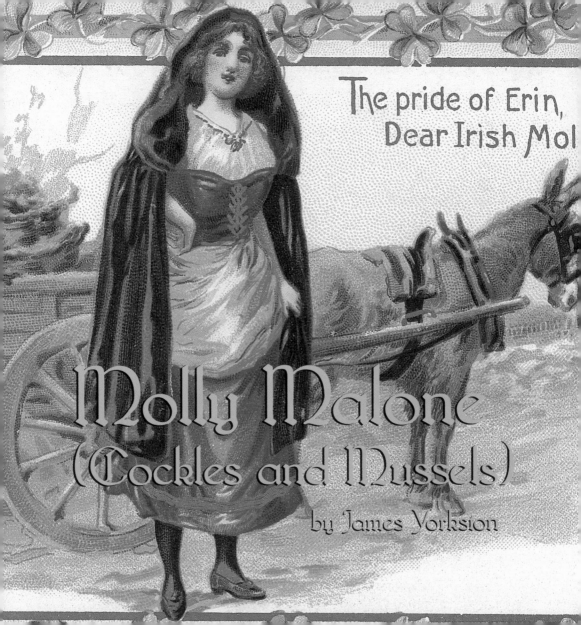

In Dublin City, where the girls they are so pretty,
'Twas there I first met with sweet Molly Malone.
She drove a wheelbarrow,
Thro' streets broad and narrow,
Crying "Cockles and mussels, alive all alive!"

> Chorus
> Alive, alive o! Alive, alive o!
> Crying "Cockles and mussels, alive all alive."

She was a fishmonger,
and that was the wonder,
Her father and mother were fishmongers too.
They drove wheelbarrows
Thro' streets broad and narrow,
Crying "Cockles and mussels, alive all alive!"

> Chorus

She died of the faver,
And nothing could save her,
And that was the end of sweet Molly Malone.
But her ghost drives a barrow,
Thro' streets broad and narrow,
Crying "Cockles and mussels, alive all alive!"

> Chorus

335

Honesty

by Máirtín
Ó Direáin

A great poet once said
an island and a woman's love
are the matter and reason
    for my poems.
It is truth you speak,
    my brother.

I'll keep the island
another while in my poem
because of the integrity
that is in stone, rock,
    and strand.

THE ORIGINAL IRISH COFFEE

According to the folks at the Irish Coffee Festival (see page 102), this drink was first concocted by chef Joe Sheridan at the Foynes Airport restaurant in 1942. As the story goes, a flight left Foynes for New York one night but, due to bad weather over the North Atlantic, had to turn back. The staff at the restaurant were told there would be cold and miserable passengers arriving, so they went to work preparing food and drink. To cheer the weary travelers up a bit, Joe thought he'd add a little drop of Irish whiskey to their coffee, and one surprised American asked, "Is this Brazilian coffee?" "No," Joe said, "that's Irish coffee."

1 shot Irish whiskey
3 sugar cubes (preferably brown)
Strong black coffee
Heavy cream, slightly whipped

1. Heat a stemmed whiskey goblet.
2. Pour in 1 shot of Irish whiskey.
3. Add 3 sugar cubes.
4. Fill with strong black coffee to within 1 inch of the top. Stir gently.
5. Top off to the brim with slightly whipped heavy cream. Add a pinch of chocolate for special occasions.

Yield: 1 serving.

Important: Do not stir after adding the cream; drink through the cream for best results!

The Four-Leafed Shamrock

by Jeremiah Curtin

This tale gives a good instance of the virtue of the four-leafed shamrock against the power which takes people's eyes—*i.e.*, true vision—from them:

A good many years ago a showman came to the town of Dingle and performed many tricks there. At one time he'd eat a dozen straws and then pull yards of ribbon from his throat. The strangest thing he showed was a game-cock that he used to harness to a great log of wood.

Men, women, and children were breaking their bones, running to see the cock, and he a small bird, drawing such a great weight of timber. One day, when the showman was driving the cock on the road toward Brandon Mountain, he met a man with a bundle of fresh grass on his back. The man was astonished to see crowds running after a cock dragging one straw behind him.

"You fool," said the people, "don't you see the cock drawing a log of timber, and it would fail any horse to draw the like of it?"

The Four-Leafed Shamrock

"Indeed, then, I do not. I see the cock dragging a straw behind him, and sure I've seen the like many a time in my own place."

Hearing this, the showman knew that there was something in the grass, and going over to the man he asked what price was he asking for the bundle. The man didn't wish to sell the grass, but at last he parted with it for eighteen pence. The showman gave the grass to his boy and told him to go aside and drop it into the river. The boy did that, and when the bundle went down with the stream the man was as big a fool as another; he ran after the cock with the crowd.

That evening the same man was telling a friend how at first he saw the cock with a straw behind him, and then saw him drawing a great log of wood. "Oh, you fool!" said the friend, "there was a four-leafed shamrock in your bundle of grass; while you had the shamrock it kept every enchantment and devilment from you, and when you parted with it, you became as big a fool as the others."

FACTS & FANCY
THE SHAMROCK

The term "Shamrock" derives from the Irish word "seamrog," which translates to "little clover," and is the common name for any of several three-leaf clovers native to Ireland. Theory holds that the druids, or ancient Celtic priests, looked at the shamrock as a sacred plant that was potent against malevolent spirits because its leaves formed a triad, three being a mystical number in the Celtic religion. In the 5th century, St Patrick used the shamrock in converting the pagan population to Christianity, citing the three leaves as symbols of the Holy Trinity, or the Father, the Son, and the Holy Spirit. However, Irish manuscripts of the time make no reference to this in connection with St Patrick, so the story is left to the realm of legend. In the 19th century, the shamrock became a symbol of Irish identity as well as rebellion against the English, anyone wearing it risking death by hanging. On the luckier side, the four-leaf clover has a long history as a lucky charm, as its pedals are often said to represent faith, hope, love, and luck. The fourth leaf is a product of genetic mutation and thought to occur in one of every 10,000 clovers. ❧

Great Irish Americans

A *pproximately 34 million Americans claim Irish ancestry, which is quite a number compared to Ireland's population of around four million! Here are a few that have made their mark on the world.*

PRESIDENTS Kennedy, Grant, Reagan, Jackson, Polk, Buchanan, Arthur, McKinley, Wilson, Nixon, and many others were of Irish descent.

DANIEL BOONE (1734–1820): Also known as Daniel Boone Reed, this American pioneer and hunter's frontier exploits and settlement of Kentucky made him one of the first US folk heroes.

CHARLES CARROLL III (1737–1832): The only Catholic to sign the Declaration of Independence, he was born in Maryland, whose laws at the time prohibited Catholics from voting, holding office, worshipping openly, or educating their children as Catholics. Despite this rampant anti-Catholic prejudice, Carroll took an active part in the American Revolution, served as a US senator in the first Congress, and when he died was reputedly the richest man in America.

DAVY CROCKETT (1786–1836): A folk hero who fought under Andrew Jackson, served Tennessee in Congress, fought in the Texas

Great Irish Americans

revolution, and died at the Battle of the Alamo.

BUFFALO BILL CODY (1846–1917): An American soldier, buffalo hunter, and showman, he was one of the most colorful figures of the Old West, famous for the shows he organized with cowboy themes.

HENRY MCCARTY (1860–1881): Also known as William H. Bonney and "Billy the Kid," this legendary gunslinger and frontier outlaw was reputed to have killed 21 men but likely killed 9. Betrayed by his friend Pat Garrett and killed, he was later immortalized by Garrett's own sensationalistic biography as well as hundreds of other books, films, magazines, and tales.

HENRY FORD (1863–1947): The son of an Irish immigrant who married during the American Civil War, he started the Ford Motor Company. Ford is now credited with the development of mass production of large numbers of inexpensive automobiles using the assembly line, coupled with high wages for his workers and a locally rooted network of franchise dealers.

NELLIE BLY (1864–1922): Also known as Elizabeth Jane Cochran, she was a pioneer of undercover journalism and a champion of women's rights, famous for committing herself to the Women's

Great Irish Americans

Lunatic Asylum on Blackwell's Island to expose its horrible conditions, as well as for traveling around the world in seventy-two days.

ÉAMON DE VALERA (1882–1975): Born in United States, he became a commandant in the 1916 Rising. His American citizenship saved him from execution. He was elected as a Sinn Fein MP for East Clare in 1917, and served as president of Ireland from 1959 to 1973.

GEORGIA O'KEEFFE (1887–1986): Widely regarded as one of the greatest painters of the 20th century, she is known for synthesizing abstraction and representation in paintings of flowers, rocks, shells, animal bones, and landscapes.

DOROTHY DAY (1897–1980): A journalist turned social activist, anarchist, and devout member of the Catholic Church, she became known for social justice campaigns in defense of the poor, forsaken, hungry, and homeless. In 1933 she founded the Catholic Worker Movement, espousing nonviolence and hospitality for the impoverished and downtrodden.

MARION MORRISON (1907–1979): Also known as John Wayne and "The Duke"—a legend of American film, largely Westerns—he is best remembered for his persona of rugged individualistic masculinity.

Irish Vocabulary

This is a list of words used in this book that most people will not be familiar with. Many are of Irish origin, although some stem from English and even French roots. Feel free to mix them with the slang on page 206 and impress the punters at your local Irish pub.

ALPEEN: a stick with a knob at the lower end

BARMBRACK: a yeast bread made with sultanas and raisins

BATTER BURGERS & CHIPS: battered and deep-fried hamburger and french fries

BOREEN: narrow country road

BROGUES: shoes made of heavy and untanned leather

CÉILITHE: social gathering where Irish songs and stories are performed

CHIPPER: the place that sells fish & chips (and batter burgers)

CHOUGH: small or medium size bird with red legs and black feathers

CODDIN': short for "codding"; hoax

COOLEEN: a maiden of fair, flowing locks

CORBEEN: a large, green, floppy beret-like cap, often worn by someone in the military

CRAIC: fun, enjoyment, good times

CRANNOG: ancient artificial island used for living or as a place of retreat

CRAYTHUR: whiskey

CROAGH: mountain/hill (also crock or knock)

CROPPY: a derogatory term for the Irish rebels of 1798, referring to their short (or cropped) hair

CRUBEENS: pig's feet

CRUISKEEN: a little pitcher for holding liquor

CURRACH (or curragh): traditional rowing boats used in the Aran Islands

DUDEEN: a short-stemmed Irish pipe

FENIAN (or Fenian king): related to the Fenian Cycle, also known as the Fionn Cycle, Finn Cycle, Fianna Cycle, or Finnian Tales—a body of prose and verse revolving around the mythic hero Fionn mac Cumhaill (more or less pronounced *Finn MacCool*) and his warriors, the Fianna Éireann

FLEADH (pronounced *flaa*): literally "festival" in Irish, it normally refers to a festival of Irish music and dance

GANSEY: a type of fisherman's sweater, traditionally hand knit by his mother, sweetheart, or wife

GORSOON: servant boy

HÉIREANN: Ireland

PUNTERS: drinkers at a pub

QUAG: soft, wet, low-lying land; bog

ROWAN: a tree with orange-red berry-like fruit

SHEILING: cottage or small shelter used by shepherds or fishermen

SLANE: a turf spade; a type of shovel to cut turf or peat

SLIEVE: a mountain

SPALPEEN: a scamp; good-for-nothing fellow

STRONGBOW: Richard "Strongbow" de Clare, along with his Welsh army of archers, is noted for beginning the Norman Conquest of Ireland

if you're enough
lucky to be irish . . .
you're lucky enough!

Acknowledgments

From *Mercier and Camier* by Samuel Beckett, copyright © 1970 by Les Editions de Minuit. This translation copyright © 1974 by Samuel Beckett. Originally published in French in © 1970 by Les Editions de Minuit, Paris, under the title *Mercier et Camier*. First published in the author's translation in 1974 in Great Britain by Calder & Boyers Ltd., London.

"After a Childhood Away from Ireland" from *An Origin Like Water: Collected Poems 1967–1987* by Eavan Boland, copyright © 1996 by Eavan Boland. Reprinted by permission of W. W. Norton & Company, Inc.

"Digging" from *Opened Ground: Selected Poems 1966–1996* by Seamus Heaney, copyright © 1998 by Seamus Heaney. Reprinted by permission of Farrar, Straus and Giroux, LLC.

"If Ever You Go to Dublin Town" by Patrick Kavanagh. Reprinted from *Collected Poems*, edited by Antoinette Quinn (Allen Lane, 2004), by kind permission of the Trustees of the Estate of the late Katherine B. Kavanagh, through the John Williams Literary Agency.

"Swans Mating" from *Selected Poems* by Michael Longley, published by Jonathan Cape, 1998. Reprinted by permission of The Random House Group Ltd and Wake Forest University Press.

From *Angela's Ashes* by Frank McCourt, copyright © 1996 by Frank McCourt. Reprinted with the permission of Scribner, an imprint of Simon & Schuster Adult Publishing Group.

From "Going Home" by Brian Moore, copyright © 1999 by Brian Moore. Orignally commissioned by *Granta* magazine in London and later appeared in *The New York Times*. Reprinted by permission of Curtis Brown, Ltd. and by permission of Farrar, Straus and Giroux, LLC

Excerpt from "Home Sickness" from *Untilled Field* by George Moore (1903; Colin Smythe Ltd, 1976). Reprinted by kind permission of Colin Smythe on behalf of the Estate of Christopher Douglas Medley.

"Do You Think Should He Have Gone Over?" from *The World: Travels 1950-2000*, copyright © 2003 Jan Morris. Reprinted by permission of W. W. Norton & Company, Inc.

"The Boundary Commission" from *Poems: 1968-1998* by Paul Muldoon, copyright © 2001 by Paul Muldoon. Reprinted by permission of Farrar, Straus and Giroux, LLC.

Excerpt from "The Long Road to Ummera" from *The Collected Stories of Frank O'Connor* by Frank O'Connor, copyright © 1981 by Harriet O'Donovan Sheehy, Executrix of the Estate of Frank O'Connor. Reprinted by permission of Alfred A. Knopf, a division of Random House, Inc.

"Honesty" by Mairtin O'Direain, translated by Maureen Murphy.

Copyright by Devin-Adair, Publishers, inc., Old Greenwich, Connecticut, 06870, Permission to reprint "Going into Exile", by Liam O'Flaherty, 1953. All rights reserved.

Illustrations

Pages 4-5: John Winsch; **10-11:** Ellen H. Clapsaddle; **15:** Cruac Padruis; **22:** H.M. Rose; **25:** W. Heath Robinson; **36:** Jessie Willcox Smith; **40-41:** Mailick; **43:** Ellen H. Clapsaddle; **44-45:** L. Herman; **50** Lang Campbell; **51:** M.W. Taggart; **52:** John Winsch; **53:** Ellen H. Clapsaddle; **63:** Monro S. Orrl; **64:** Willy Pogány; **75:** Warwick Goble; **56:** John Winsch; **76:** Ellen H. Clapsaddle; **82:** Harry G. Theaker; **87:** John Winsch; **88:** Ellen H. Clapsaddle; **93:** R. Veentliet; **104:** Paus; **106-107:** Maurice C. Wilks; **109:** Ellen H. Clapsaddle; **128:** John Carey; **140-141:** John Winsch; 152 C.E.B. Bernard; **202:** Harry G. Theaker; **215:** Warwick Goble; **240-241:** H.B.G.; **255:** John Winsch; **267:** John Winsch; **285:** Aleinmüller; **293:** John Winsch; **301:** Ellen H. Clapsaddle; **309:** John Winsch; **323:** Monro S. Orr; **338:** Mailick.

Thanks to the *wee folk* for their enormous help:

Aunt Eileen, Aunt Joan, Aunt Sheila, Daneen Quirk Cali, Diarmaid, Grandma Foley, Guy, Jeanne, Alannah, Finn & Tighe, Kathryn Hayes, Ann Hogan Liberator Jimenez, Marie Mayhew, Mary Foley Measom, Brendan Rayment, Sheila Sullivan, Uncle Peter & Aunt Kay.